"Be careful!" Papa yelled as I pulled myself up on top of the wall and dangled my feet over the side.

It was scary to be up so high, staring down at the wide blue sea. But I took a deep breath and felt a little braver.

I thought of you, Malka, and Mama and Bubbe and my brothers, how far you all still are from us. I wanted to stretch out my arms and give you a hug. But my sorrows were mixed with my joys. The sea was calm and peaceful and seemed to be whispering to me, *I will bring your family to you. Soon, soon, soon.*

Sending you all my love,
Esther

Also by Ruth Behar

Lucky Broken Girl

LETTERS FROM CUBA

RUTH BEHAR

NANCY PAULSEN BOOKS

NANCY PAULSEN BOOKS
An imprint of Penguin Random House LLC, New York

First published in the United States of America by Nancy Paulsen Books,
an imprint of Penguin Random House LLC, 2020
First paperback edition published 2021

Visit us online at penguinrandomhouse.com

THE LIBRARY OF CONGRESS HAS CATALOGED THE HARDCOVER EDITION AS FOLLOWS:
Names: Behar, Ruth, 1956– author.
Title: Letters from Cuba / Ruth Behar.
Description: New York: Nancy Paulsen Books, [2020] | Includes bibliographical references. |
Summary: In 1938, eleven-year-old Esther joins her father in tropical, multicultural Cuba, where they toil together to rescue the rest of their Jewish family from persecution in Poland. Includes notes about the author's grandmother, on whom the story is based.
Identifiers: LCCN 2020009211 | ISBN 9780525516477 (hardcover) |
ISBN 9780525516484 (ebook)
Subjects: CYAC: Refugees—Fiction. | Immigrants—Fiction. | Jews—Cuba—Fiction. |
Dressmaking—Fiction. | Cuba—History—1933–1959—Fiction. | Letters—Fiction.
Classification: LCC PZ7.1.B447 Let 2020 | DDC [Fic]—dc23
LC record available at https://lccn.loc.gov/2020009211

Printed in the United States of America

ISBN 9780525516491

1 3 5 7 9 10 8 6 4 2

Design by Eileen Savage
Text set in Winchester New ITC

In memory of my Baba and her Baba

"For how can I bear to see disaster fall on my people?
How can I bear to see the destruction of my family?"

Esther 8:6

Yo vengo de todas partes,
Y hacia todas partes voy:
Arte soy entre las artes,
En los montes, monte soy.

I come from many places,
And to every place I go:
I am art among the arts,
And mountain among mountains.

José Martí, *Versos sencillos*
(*Simple Verses*), 1891

LETTERS FROM CUBA

GOVOROVO

December 2, 1937

Dearest Papa,

I am writing to you out of desperation. I pray that my letter arrives safely in your hands so you will listen to my plea.

How is it possible we're still separated from you and that three years have passed since you left for Cuba? Would you recognize us today—your own family?

I could fill a river with my tears when I think of you being so far away. Mama worries we will never see you again. "Your papa is gone forever," she says. She scares my brothers and sister with those terrible words, but I promise them we'll be reunited.

You will be surprised to learn how much I've grown in the last year. I'm taller than Mama now (which I know isn't saying much). I try to do everything I can to help here. I go to the woods every day and cut balls of juniper for cooking. After school, I work two afternoons a week for Yoelke the baker, sweeping ashes and crumbs. He pays me with two loaves of rye bread so that for breakfast we have something to dip into the bit of milk our tired cow, Zisseleh, still gives us.

The other children help as much as they can, especially Malka. She reminds me of you because she's smart and studious and never complains. Every morning she warms the water for Bubbe so it won't be too cold when she washes up. Even the twins are old enough to help—you wouldn't recognize Eliezer and Chaim, since they were such babies when you left for Cuba. Today they collected three full buckets of berries with Moshe, who they look up to and call "Little Papa." This made Mama smile. She is beautiful when she smiles and her blue eyes sparkle.

I'm sad to say not a lot makes Mama smile anymore. It's getting harder and harder for us here in Poland, especially for me and Moshe and the twins, since we all share your dark hair and eyes. There is no chance we can pass for Polish as Mama and Malka often can. The Poles always know we are Jews. Some are kind, but some give us nasty looks and spit on the ground as we walk past. Yet I've seen them nod hello to Mama and Malka, as if they are more worthy, just because of how they look.

Mama is still angry about the loss of our store in Govorovo, and what happened was so unfair. Now that I'm older, I understand that the government overtaxed you and put you out of business just because we are Jewish. You had no choice but to leave Poland to find work and take care of all of us. I don't know what we'd do without the money you send us from Cuba.

I've been thinking a lot about all this. According to Jewish tradition, I will be an adult when I turn twelve in a few months.

The truth shouldn't be kept from me, which is why I'm upset that Mama tried to hide your letter. She knows how much I miss you, and I am always asking if you've written. I thought we hadn't heard from you in so long because the mail's unreliable these days, but then I found your letter squirreled away inside her shoe. I had gotten suspicious because suddenly we had a little bit of meat to eat with our potatoes and the money had to come from somewhere.

When I read your letter, I understood why Mama hid it. She didn't want me to know that you now have enough savings to bring only one of us to Cuba. Papa, you write that the child who should travel first is Moshe because he's the oldest of the boys and you think he'll be the most capable of helping you work. But I'm the eldest and stronger than you think. By birthright, it is I who should come. Please, Papa, choose me. Don't think less of me because I am a girl. I will help you show Mama that it wasn't a mistake for you to go to Cuba. I promise if you let me be the one to come first, I will work hard and make you proud.

I'm eager to see you, dear Papa, and hear your voice. Put your trust in me. I will not disappoint you.

Your loving daughter,
Esther

ON BOARD THE SHIP TO CUBA

January 22, 1938

Dear Malka,

Oh dear sister, I have been on the ship for three days and three nights and I still keep pinching myself, unable to believe I'm really on my way to Cuba! Even after I begged, I doubted Papa would choose me. I'm so grateful, but saying goodbye at the train station was the hardest thing I've ever done.

The tears in Bubbe's eyes left a hole in my heart. When she wiped my tears with her embroidered handkerchief, then gave it to me as a gift, I could barely hold myself together. I was surprised to see some tears from Moshe, Eliezer, and Chaim too. I guess they will miss me a little. Mama will too, I hope. I was touched when she gave me her silver thimble to remember her by, even though I know she's still angry with me for encouraging Papa to go to Cuba—but where else was he to go when the door to the United States had closed to Jewish refugees? I hugged her and told her I loved her, and all she said was "Tell your father we need him at home."

But you, Malka, my treasured only sister, I know you will miss me as much as I'll miss you. I feel terrible that I won't be around to protect you at school. I hope you'll feel like I'm there in spirit, urging you to stay smart and studious, even when jealous girls tease you. And if one of them hides your eyeglasses again, please tell Moshe!

I don't know what I will do without you and I'll be thinking of you every day. I promise to write down every interesting thing that happens while we're apart so that the hours, weeks, and months we're separated won't seem so painful. I'm beginning now, writing in this old accounting notebook of Papa's, and I will fill it up with letters from Cuba that I will save for you. Writing them will make the days bearable until you arrive. Then when you're finally here, we will read them together and it will be as if you were with me the whole time.

The train ride from Warsaw to Rotterdam was scary. I worried if I got up to go to the bathroom, another traveler would take my seat. I sat stiff as a doll and ate the hard-boiled egg you packed for me and barely had a sip of water. Mama had warned me to be careful around strangers, so I looked at no one and kept my eyes glued to the window. I felt happy and sad at the same time, seeing my own country as I was leaving it behind. Glimpses of cities, towns, and forests that I would never know flew past. If only things were different for us in Poland and we hadn't lost our store! If only so many people didn't hate us. If only, if only . . . My head grew heavy from holding back the tears. But if I started crying, I wouldn't stop!

When we crossed the border from Germany into the Netherlands, they ordered everyone who had steamship tickets to step down from the train. We had to walk a long way to get to the inspection station, where we were checked for illnesses and had our baggage disinfected. The doctor hardly examined me at all, quickly looking down my throat and running his fingers over my scalp. But there were grown-ups who weren't so lucky, and they wouldn't be allowed to continue their journey.

"But here's my steamship ticket! My brother's waiting for me!" a man yelled in a mix of Polish and Yiddish. He lifted his suitcase onto his shoulders and shoved his way toward the door. A policeman rushed after him and dragged him back in. The man's suit got torn and his nose spouted blood as he crumpled to the ground. I felt so sad. With his dark beard, the man reminded me of Papa. I went to his side and offered him the handkerchief that Bubbe gave me. He brightened and smiled at me. "Shayna maideleh, shayna maideleh," he said in a gentle voice. "You are a beautiful dear maiden, just like my daughter at home."

He told me his name was Jacob. At first, Jacob wouldn't take the handkerchief. He said he didn't want to dirty it, but I told him I wanted him to have it, that it was my grandmother's gift and she'd be proud of me for helping him. By then it was night. All the people there, whether they'd passed the inspection or not, had nowhere to go, and they slept on the floor or leaning against the walls. I stayed with Jacob and felt safe enough to sleep. In the morning, we said our goodbyes and he held my head with both hands and gave me his blessing: "May you go in peace to your destination and be delivered from accidents and enemies along the way."

I returned to the station and took the train to Rotterdam, feeling less afraid because of Jacob's blessing. And do you know what? I think it protected me. When I arrived in Rotterdam, I noticed an old couple speaking Yiddish. The man had a white beard and wore the black suit of a rabbi, and the woman's hair was hidden under a kerchief. I asked if they knew the directions to the port, and it turned out they had tickets for the same ship as me!

"What are you doing alone, little girl?" the woman asked.

"I am not little. I am fifteen," I told them. All the papers say I am fifteen, so I thought I'd better keep my story straight, though I felt bad about lying to them. But then I told them the truth. "There was only enough money for one child to travel, so I'm going to help my father bring all our family to Cuba."

"It's a shame we are being forced out of our home," the old woman said.

"We didn't want to leave Poland," the old man added. "We've lived all our lives there and our ancestors are buried in that soil. But it's changed. Our children are in Mexico and it's time for us to join them."

I became worried. "But how can we be on the same ship? My ticket says it's for Cuba."

They assured me the ship would make several stops, and we set off together toward the port. Since I only had a small bag for my few necessities, I carried the woman's heavy suitcase. Before the ocean came into view, I could feel the change in the air, and flocks of white birds appeared. They circled the sky and sang a wistful tune. I learned they were seagulls! A moment later, I saw the ocean and could not believe how huge it was! Extending to the edge of the world.

We found our ship at the dock but had to pass yet another medical exam before we could board. The old couple gave me some of their herring and potatoes or I would not have eaten. Then when they came to check our passports, my heart was thumping so loudly I was afraid a policeman would rush aboard the ship and pull me off. I wanted to set sail right away, not wait another moment. But I'm learning that everything in life happens in its own good time.

Now we are out on the high seas and there's nothing but water surrounding us. In the morning, the ocean is blue, in the afternoon, it is green, and in the evening, it is purple. I'm grateful I've seen the miracle of the ocean. If I died tomorrow, I would be happy I've seen it. But I don't plan on dying. I have to get to Cuba!

What takes more getting used to is the sound of the waves. Sometimes it is like the whisper of a lullaby, soft and soothing. But when the wind blows hard, the crashing waves sound like the roar of a lion. That's when my fears about this journey become difficult to shoo away. I am crossing the ocean. But it feels as if the ocean is crossing me.

Your sister, who misses you,

Esther

ON BOARD THE SHIP TO CUBA

January 26, 1938

Dearest sister Malka,

I'm sure there are magnificent ships in the world, but this is not one of them. This ship is crowded and dirty and smells of rotten meat and vomit. People say the ship is too old and shouldn't be traveling the seas anymore. I'm in steerage, which is where the poorest passengers are squeezed together. I have a berth with a straw mattress, and my life preserver is my pillow.

I share the compartment with a group of Jewish women who are soon-to-be brides. Their fiancés—whom they've never met—await them in Mexico. We share a washroom and lavatory, and two women always stand guard when other women are using it. We have to share the soap and even the towels and washcloths. When we boarded the ship, we were each given a spoon, a fork, a tin plate, and a tin pail—to be used for both eating and as a washbasin. So you can imagine how hard it is to stay clean!

Rita, the bride-to-be who sleeps in the bunk bed below mine, told me that their fiancés are not obligated to marry them if they find their brides-to-be unattractive. She's worried because her face has broken out with pimples. "What if I'm left in the street all by myself?" she asks. "What will become of me?" She cries every night and extends her hand up toward my bed, and I hold on to it until she falls asleep. Oh, dear little sister, I am glad I am too young to think of marriage and that I am promised to no one but myself!

The weather's been cold and stormy, and the blanket the ship provided is thin as gauze. I use my ragged winter coat as a second blanket. I haven't stepped out on the deck these last two days. Those of us in steerage only get to enjoy a small corner of the deck anyway.

From our deck, we can see the enormous deck of the first-class passengers, where elegantly dressed people relax on lounge chairs and waiters serve them drinks on trays. Yesterday, a mother in steerage took her sick baby up there so he could get fresh air and they shouted at her to go back to where she belonged. That night I couldn't sleep, thinking about what had happened and how helpless that woman must have felt. Why does such injustice exist? How did it come about that some people are rich and others poor?

Meals are terrible too. There's rye bread, but it's not soft and chewy like Yoelke's bread in Govorovo. It's hard as a brick and must be soaked in tea or it will break your teeth. We also get watery pea soup and old potatoes. The meat tastes like shoe leather, but they say it's kosher. All I can hold in my stomach are sweet things—tea laced with sugar cubes and the coffee cakes they offer in the afternoon. Maybe it is my body's way of preparing me for the sugar fields of Cuba!

Sorry to be complaining so much. I guess that's the thing about writing. Once you start, all kinds of thoughts and feelings spill out! But I did keep the best news for last—the other day I was roaming the aisles of the ship and heard what sounded like mooing. I followed the sound and found stables filled with cows, sheep, and goats. It felt as if I'd stumbled onto Noah's ark! I greeted the animals and they looked at me with the saddest eyes. Then I heard footsteps coming up behind me. It was a young sailor I'd seen mopping the floors in steerage. His name is Casper and he's Dutch but speaks some Polish. I thought he'd scold me, but instead he smiled.

"Do you like the animals?" he asked.

"Yes," I told him. "And I feel sorry they can't wander around the ship. They must hate being trapped in here. They don't see the light of the sun. Poor things."

"I know what you mean. They suffer during the journey. But please don't tell anyone you have seen the animals. It is a secret they are down here."

He let me help him arrange fresh hay for the cows, goats, and sheep.

Then Casper showed me a picture of his wife that he keeps in his pocket. He held his palm against his heart to show me how much he misses her. The life of a sailor and his wife must be difficult, being far apart for so long. Now I too am like a sailor, far from everyone I love.

I would be so miserable on this ship if not for Casper letting me come back each day to help with the animals. There's a soft, cuddly baby lamb that I get to hold as long as I like. When I hug the lamb, I realize how much I miss you, sweet sister, and my beloved bubbe. And I miss my dear angry mother and even my brothers, who might miss me a little? With the baby lamb in my arms, I have faith I will make it to dry land and you'll hear good news from me.

Your older sister,
who loves you very much,
Esther

PORT OF MÉRIDA

February 1, 1938

Dearest Malka,

A cry of joy rose from the deck when we approached land! I rushed to join Rita and her friends as they gathered around the railing. Today I will see Papa, I thought. Today I will kiss his cheek and feel the tickle of his dark beard. Today I will begin a new life in Cuba! But then I learned we had arrived in Mexico first, not in Cuba, as everyone had expected. The port city I was seeing was Mérida, not Havana. How much longer would I have to wait to be reunited with Papa? Why must everything take so long?

I pushed past people to return to steerage, where I could sulk by myself. On my way, I bumped into the kind old couple who had shared their herring and potatoes with me in Rotterdam. They both looked pale and weakened from the journey, even though they had made the voyage in first class.

"One more day on this rotten ship and I would not have survived," the old woman moaned.

The old man added, "A day is a lifetime, and being on the ship for all these days felt like I used up several lifetimes."

"But wasn't it worth it?" I asked them. "You will see your children at last!"

The old woman looked so sad. "Of what use will we be to them? I hope we are not a burden. But we are here and there is no turning back now."

"I am certain your children love you deeply and are waiting eagerly to place a kiss on your cheeks. Your presence will be a blessing to them," I said.

The old man smiled. "You are very wise for such a young girl. And I see you have no bitterness in your heart." He reached inside his black suit and pulled out a gold pocket watch.

The old woman gasped. "Hershel, what are you doing?"

"I know what I am doing, Bluma," he replied sharply. Then he turned to me. "Child, this is my gift to you. I know our paths will never cross again. We will stay in Mexico and you will go on to Cuba. But even long after you have forgotten our chance encounter, hold on to this watch, and may it bless you with many hours of happiness and hope."

I hesitated to accept such a precious gift. "Thank you, but if I take this from you, how will you tell the time?"

He pressed the pocket watch into my hand. "Child, you cannot refuse this gift. I want you to have it. I am old and do not have many years left. You have all the time in the world before you."

I stared at the Roman numerals, then I closed the clasp. It's good I wear dresses with deep pockets on both sides. I slipped the watch into my right pocket to have it handy. When I looked up, the old man and his wife had disappeared into the crowd.

One by one, all the passengers got off in Mérida. Rita was the last to leave, and I gave her a hug. She was so afraid of what her fiancé would think of her. I hope she won't end up like a stray dog roaming the streets of Mexico.

I returned to steerage, until a policeman came to check if anyone was still on board. When he spotted me in my berth, he said, "Vamos."

I didn't know what that meant, so I shook my head and said, "Cuba, Cuba."

He laughed and said, "México, México." I showed him my ticket, pointed to where it said Cuba.

He sighed and walked away, then came back with Casper. Between the two of them, they explained: The animals are going on to Cuba, and I would be the only human passenger going with them. We'd set sail the next day. "Mañana," as the policeman said. Tomorrow.

I felt such desperation all alone on the ship, wanting so badly to get off and set foot on dry land. I cannot describe how huge my sorrow was that day. May you never know such sorrow, dear Malka, to be so far from everyone you care about.

Soon after, Casper returned with fresh hay for the animals, and he brought me a marvelous gift—a cluster of bananas! He saw me about to bite into the thick yellow outer crust and quickly stopped me and showed me how to peel it and eat only the soft, creamy fruit inside. It was delicious! I couldn't stop and ate one after another. The bananas filled me up, and I thought if there were nothing else to eat ever again, I could live on bananas for a long time.

With love always from
your older sister,
Esther

PORT OF HAVANA

February 4, 1938

Dearest Malka,

I awoke and it was still dark out. I looked in on the animals. They were sleeping peacefully, except the lamb, who looked up at me and seemed to say, "We're almost there."

I washed up and then packed my things and put on the dress that was a little cleaner, tucking the pocket watch away on the right side. I wanted to be ready to dash into Papa's arms as soon as we docked in Havana.

I climbed to the deck and looked out at the sea. The air was warm and comforting like a bowl of soup. There was the slightest sliver of a moon. Then I heard wings flapping. I heard that wistful song and knew it was a seagull. A Cuban seagull! I could not yet see firm land, but I was getting closer. The seagull had come to tell me.

The sailors and stewards came up from their rooms and stood next to me on the deck. Casper arrived, carrying the baby lamb, which he placed in my arms. Soon a shrine came into view. "¡La Virgen de Regla!" they yelled. Casper and the other sailors looked out toward the shrine and bowed their heads in prayer. I heard them thanking the Virgin for bringing them safely to Cuba. I had arrived with Jacob's blessing, the man who looked like Papa whom I met on the way to Rotterdam. I hope he crossed the border and is on his way to being reunited with his brother.

We came into the port just as the first rays of the sun bathed the city in a soft pink glow. I looked every which way, taking in the beauty of Havana. It was not a jungle at all, despite what Mama always says! A flash of light drew my eyes to the other side of the bay, where a tall lighthouse stood by a stone castle perched high on a crag. I turned back to face the city and saw mansions lining the coast and, in the distance, a huge building with many columns and a golden dome reflecting the rising sun. Two fishermen on a small rowboat held up a big fish they'd caught and waved to us.

As we approached the pier, Casper took the lamb from me to bring her back to her mother in the stable, and that was the last I saw of her. I hope the lamb and the rest of the animals will go to a farm somewhere in Cuba with green pastures and sunny hillsides where they will feast on grasses and flowers and never be trapped again in the dark belly of a ship. I hope that I too will only see the light of day from now on.

With all my love,
your sister,
ESTHER

TRISCORNIA

February 4, 1938

My dear sweet Malka,

As soon as we landed in Havana and the ship was being secured with thick ropes, a policeman appeared and whisked me onto a small boat. He spoke to me in Spanish and I didn't understand a word.

"Papa, Papa," I said. He shook his head and I began to cry. Where was he taking me? How would Papa know where to find me?

I soon learned that on the other side of the harbor is a place called Triscornia, where they bring immigrants. In a crowded office that smelled of sweat, a health inspector checked my hair for lice and made sure I didn't have a cough while a policeman looked through my things. Then they pointed to a chair in a corner. It was next to an open window, and the strong wind that blew in felt like it could lift me into the air and take me back to Poland. But I was far, far away now. I sat down and started writing to you, hoping that putting words on the page would calm my worries and bring Papa to me. I hoped nothing bad had happened to him. Otherwise I'd be in the same situation that poor Rita had feared if her fiancé didn't like her—all alone in a foreign land.

After a while, they shooed me outside. That was when I discovered I wasn't the only Jewish refugee in Triscornia. As I walked around the fenced-in yard, I heard Yiddish being spoken and learned there were people who'd been here for months. They had illnesses they caught on the journey, or their families hadn't yet come for them, or they didn't have money for the entrance fee that the government requires. Their clothes were dirty and wrinkled and hung heavily on their bodies in the tropical heat. They looked lost among the lost. They were in Cuba but could not enter Cuba. How horrible to make such a long journey and end up stuck in a camp with other helpless refugees!

I said hello to a group of men and women sitting on blankets in the shade. They greeted me in Yiddish, and I decided to entertain them with the story of my journey.

I rose to my feet and began to speak as if I were on a stage.

"I crossed the ocean on a ship that was like Noah's ark—full of cows and sheep and goats. There was a baby lamb too. The Dutch sailor who took care of the animals let me cuddle with the baby lamb every day. That's what kept me from losing faith on my journey."

"That's impossible!" a man said. "They don't bring animals aboard the ships that are carrying immigrants."

A woman added, “The animals would create a big stinky mess. No one would tolerate it!”

“You’re a good storyteller,” another woman said.

Then the man spoke to me in a nicer voice. “Child, are you sure you didn’t imagine all those animals?”

“I saw the animals every day. They were in a secret corridor. No one knew except me. The animals didn’t bother anyone. They were my companions.”

“If you say so, child, if you say so. Maybe it was all a dream that was so vivid it seemed real.”

“It was not a dream! I saw the animals with my own eyes and I held the baby lamb in my own arms!”

“Yes, child, of course.”

I was enraged. Why didn’t they believe me?

“It’s true, it’s true!” I shouted.

“What is true, dear one? Can you tell me?”

I looked up, and there was Papa, holding his arms open toward me! I was so shocked I couldn’t speak. I sunk into his embrace. Tears flowed from his eyes and from my eyes. They were all the tears I’d held in the three years we’d been apart.

“Papa, Papa! You found me!”

“Of course, my Esther.”

Papa still had his kind smile and playful wink, but he was thinner and worry lines creased his brow. His beard was gone too.

He reached into his satchel and pulled out a loaf of challah and a cluster of bananas to share with the group.

"There is challah in Cuba, Papa?"

"Here in Havana there is. There are Jews from all over Europe, and they have a very good Jewish bakery, La Flor de Berlín. Enjoy the challah, my friends. And Shabbat Shalom."

I had forgotten it was Friday and the Sabbath would start at dusk. Together we said the prayer for the challah and then the Shehecheyanu blessing to celebrate our new beginning. The challah was rich with eggs, and the bananas were even sweeter than the ones I had in Mexico.

Then Papa and I got ready to leave. He had an official-looking document that was covered in stamps and seals, as well as the letter I had written begging him to let me come to Cuba first. He also had a picture of him and Mama with the five of us children taken in Govorovo before he came to Cuba. He showed these things to one of the immigration officers at Triscornia to prove he was my father. The man held up my letter, turning it this way and that, trying to make sense of it. He asked Papa what language it was written in. Papa said it was Yiddish and that it was from me, his stubborn daughter, who wanted to come to Cuba. The man smiled at me and said, "Bienvenida," which I learned meant "Welcome."

Passing through the gate with Papa, I turned and waved to the people who were stuck in Triscornia, wondering if they would ever get out.

I am learning how difficult it is to cross borders. Misfortune or illness can leave a person stranded with nowhere to go.

I gripped Papa's hand and felt blessed that I had arrived safely and we'd found each other. That is a miracle, isn't it?

With love from your older sister,
who always remembers you,
Esther

ON THE TRAIN FROM HAVANA TO MATANZAS

February 4, 1938

Dearest Malka,

Papa said he'd take me to see a little bit of Havana. Then we'd go to the small town where he lived because the rent was cheaper than in the city.

We climbed aboard a ferry that went from Triscornia to the port of Havana. Papa had his satchel and I carried my bag and ragged winter coat. It was hot—my dress stuck to my body like a postage stamp and my legs burned inside my woolen stockings. I looked around at the women and girls on the ferry; they wore dresses that were as thin as tissue paper, showing their arms. Their legs were also uncovered, and their feet, in sandals, were visible to everyone. The men wore loose pants and light suit jackets. Some wore long shirts with pockets down the front that they did not tuck into their pants. Papa wore a black suit and a white shirt as always, but the cloth was a thinner material than what he used to wear in Poland. I stayed close to Papa, listening to the sprightly rhythm of Spanish words being spoken all around us. Everyone nodded in a polite way in my direction, and I wondered if it was because I stood out with my pale skin and woolen clothing. On the ferry, there were people with darker skin than I'd ever seen in Poland.

Papa grasped my elbow and whispered to me in Yiddish, "We're almost there, Esther. Now, don't be staring so much. That's not polite."

"I'm not staring, Papa. I'm admiring the beautiful faces of the people!"

Papa smiled and gave my shoulders a squeeze. "You've always been very curious, my daughter. It's so good you are here. I feel fortunate my prayers were answered and you arrived safely."

"Me too. I can't even believe I'm in Cuba and we're riding together on a ferry! But, Papa, you never used to travel on the eve of the Sabbath."

"I know, Esther. But we're in Cuba now and must adjust to the style of life here. As you can see, I have shaved off my beard. But I still pray every morning and evening. And I still carry the prayer book I received when I was a boy." He pulled the worn book from his pocket to show me.

That reminded me about what I had in my pocket. I pulled out the gold watch and it shone in the sun.

"Look, Papa, an old man who was traveling with his wife on the same ship gave me his pocket watch as a gift. He said I was wise for my age."

"That was a generous gift. But don't be showing it off in the streets of Havana. There are excellent pickpockets here and they'll snatch it right out of your hand. Now, let's go."

I pushed the watch deeper into my pocket and followed Papa off the ferry. We had arrived at the port of Havana. The wide avenue along the coastline was filled with people strolling back and forth as if they hadn't a care in the world.

"This avenue is called the Malecón," Papa told me.

I repeated the word in my head to remember it.

"Papa, let's go for a stroll!" I said.

"I'm sorry, there's no time," Papa replied. "We have two trains to catch and I have to take care of some business first."

Papa led me across the busy avenue and through a maze of streets, holding my hand as he used to do when I was little. We were soon in a leafy plaza where people sat on benches reading newspapers and street peddlers sold roasted peanuts. We passed cafés that opened to the street where women in wide straw hats sipped coffee from tiny cups. A pleasant smoky scent filled the air. Papa told me it was from the cigars made from the fine tobacco leaves that grow in Cuba. We kept walking through the narrow streets and wide plazas, till we came to the largest plaza of all.

Peddlers stood around with fruit carts. My mouth was watering. But I didn't have to ask Papa. He got me a wedge of pineapple, which is "piña"in Spanish, with the curlicue over the *n*. Though on the outside it looks like a large scratchy pine cone, on the inside there is a delicious, juicy, sweet fruit. When the peddler woman saw how much I enjoyed the pineapple, she gave me a cone made from a dried palm leaf filled with a thick paste of coconut and brown sugar. It's called a "cucurucho de coco"—isn't that beautiful? The coconut was crunchy and milky and sweet too.

Papa reached into his pocket for change, but she wouldn't let him pay for it. He told me to say "Gracias," which means "Thank you." It was my first time speaking Spanish!

The woman cheered and said, "Una polaquita linda."

I asked Papa what that meant and he said, "A pretty little Polish girl." He explained that in Cuba they call all Jews by that name—"polacos," or Polish people, which is funny, since in Poland they call us Jews and don't think we're really Polish.

Then the woman gave me a hug as if she'd known me forever. Dear Malka, I fell in love with Cuba at that moment!

But we had no time to dawdle. Papa said we needed to keep going. He led me across the plaza to a long street crowded with stores selling fabric, silks, leather goods, women's clothes, and men's ties and shirts.

"This is Calle Muralla. All these stores are owned by Jewish immigrants," Papa said. "They are the lucky ones. They have more customers than they can handle. But they have no choice but to work on the Sabbath. It's the busiest shopping day."

We entered a small, dusty store filled with boxes of all shapes and sizes. There was hardly room to stand. The store owner, a big man with a booming voice, welcomed Papa warmly in Yiddish.

"Avrum, so your daughter is finally here from Poland! And what a shayna maideleh she is."

In my sweaty clothes, I didn't feel like a pretty maiden.

The man smiled and said, "Don't be shy. Tell me, what is your name?"

"I am Esther."

"Well, Esther, I am Zvi Mandelbaum. I'm from a town not far from Govorovo. Now that you are in Cuba, your feet must be swollen in those lace-up shoes." He pointed behind me. "See that room in the back of the store? Go take off your stockings, and when you return, we'll find you some comfortable sandals. You give her permission, don't you, Avrum?"

"It is hot and she's in Cuba. What choice do I have?"

I went to the back room and felt glad to have permission to remove the itchy stockings. But I also felt embarrassed at the thought of my bare legs and feet being visible to Papa and Zvi Mandelbaum. There was a full-length mirror hanging on the wall. I looked at myself and saw a different girl from the one who boarded the ship in Rotterdam. I was in Cuba, and my legs and feet and ten toes needed to breathe!

When I returned to the front of the store, Zvi Mandelbaum had arranged several pairs of sandals around a chair.

"Try these on. Let's see what fits."

I didn't have to try on all the sandals. The first pair, made of soft brown leather, was perfect.

Zvi Mandelbaum wouldn't let Papa pay for my sandals.

"How can I charge you for the sandals, Avrum? You're helping me so much with sales in the countryside. I admire all of you peddlers who are willing to go deep into the hills of Cuba where there's not another Jew for miles and miles."

Zvi Mandelbaum towered over Papa as he placed his arm around Papa's shoulders. "Come now," he told Papa. "Let me give you a few more things to sell and we will both make some money."

Papa disappeared into another private room with Zvi Mandelbaum. He returned with his satchel stuffed to the brim. When I saw Papa bent over from the weight of his bag, I said, "Papa, I didn't know you were a peddler. I thought you owned a store."

"I do own a store, Esther. I carry it on my back."

"What do you sell, Papa? Let me see."

"Not now, Esther. We have a train to catch. I'll show you when we get home."

"Goodbye, Esther. Enjoy your sandals," Zvi Mandelbaum said as we left his store.

Even with the satchel on his back, Papa could walk fast, and I hurried to keep up. He pointed out some of the landmarks of the city, which made me sorry to be leaving so soon. "See, that's the Parque Central! The statue in the middle is José Martí. He was a poet and independence leader. Cubans adore him. Don't ever say anything bad about him to anyone." And then he pointed to the building I had seen from the ship. "That domed building is the Capitolio. It looks like the American Capitol in Washington, but larger and more spectacular, so they say here."

We arrived at the station and Papa got our tickets. He said we would go to a large town called Matanzas and from there we'd catch another train to a small town called Agramonte. It won't be as magnificent as Havana, but it will be home, and it will be beautiful because I will be with Papa. I would go with him to the ends of the earth.

Poor Papa was so tired he fell asleep as soon as the train started chugging along. He's snoring as I write to you. Dear Malka, I imagine you're reading a book, Moshe is studying Talmud and complaining, the twins are wrestling, Mama is sewing, and Bubbe is embroidering another special handkerchief.

I am getting sleepy like Papa, so I will write more on the next train.

Your sister, who loves
you very much,
ESTHER

ON THE TRAIN FROM MATANZAS TO AGRAMONTE

February 4, 1938

My dear sister!

I ended up taking a long nap together with Papa on the first train from Havana to Matanzas. It felt so good to curl up next to him and not be alone anymore! We might have kept on sleeping, but thankfully we were startled awake by the slamming of the brakes as the train pulled into the station in Matanzas.

Everyone rushed to get off the train. For a moment, I was separated from Papa and I fell into a panic. "Papa, Papa!" I yelled, unable to find him.

People turned and asked, "Niña, ¿qué pasa?" which I later learned meant "Little girl, what's wrong?" Cubans didn't look at me with hatred in their eyes. It was the strangest sensation to realize I was no longer in Poland, where the word "Jew" hung on the lips of strangers like a curse.

A few steps ahead, Papa came into view. I ran to him and everyone around me smiled.

We sat on a bench in the station to wait for our next train. It was late in the afternoon and the warm air had thickened like porridge. I was glad I'd taken off my stockings in Havana. I hope I can find a bit of cloth to make myself a lighter dress.

All the girls and women here wear sleeveless dresses. It's not proper for Jewish girls in Poland, but the Cuban heat is very strong, so I don't think Papa will mind.

Papa pulled out more challah and bananas from his satchel for a snack. We said the prayer again before we ate. "If you eat without thanking God, you are no better than a beast," Papa told me. He cut up slices of the challah with his pocketknife and we ate it gratefully with the bananas.

I couldn't help asking, "Papa, did you miss us all these years?"

He sounded so sad when he answered, "Of course I missed you. I don't know how three years slipped by so quickly. It feels like I arrived in Cuba only yesterday. And after working so hard, I've only managed to bring you to Cuba, while my dear wife, my mother, and my four other children suffer in Poland. I'm a terrible failure."

"Please don't think that way, Papa. I'm here now to help."

Papa sighed. "I am glad you've come, Esther. I think Cuba agrees with you. Now let's see what you think of Agramonte."

The next train arrived and we climbed aboard. It was a smaller train filled with people in dusty clothes and shoes, their hands rough and callused.

"They are sugarcane workers," Papa explained. "There are many sugar mills around here. They cut the cane with machetes and boil it to make the molasses that becomes sugar. The work is bitter, but the result is sweet."

We both stayed awake, sitting side by side, gazing at the

sugarcane fields that dotted the landscape. The cane grows tall and forms huge thickets that dance in the breeze. Leaving Matanzas, the train moved on a track parallel to the river. Then it curved around and turned into some tree-covered hills. It reminded me a little of the forest between Govorovo and Vishkov, but with tall palm trees instead—can you imagine?!

The train stopped at lots of little villages, then there was one big one called Unión de Reyes. One side of the track was filled with sturdy wooden houses where the better-off people must live, and on the other side, there were rickety shacks, probably where the peasants who cut the sugarcane live.

At last we stopped at a station with a sign that read AGRAMONTE. It was a town no bigger than Govorovo! I said I would follow Papa to the ends of the earth and I have done just that. Now I will finish writing to you, beloved sister. It is time to know my new home in Cuba.

With love from Cuba,

ESTHER

AGRAMONTE

February 6, 1938

Dearest Malka,

The countryside is so alive in Cuba! On my first night in our little wooden house, I fell asleep to the sound of crickets chattering in the darkness, then woke to the brightest sunshine I've ever seen and birds singing and roosters crowing so loudly it seemed they were right next to me.

But I was afraid. "Papa!" I called. "Papa, where are you?"

There was no reply, and I sat on the edge of my bed and whispered, "Mama, Mama." I wanted to hear Mama's voice breaking open the morning. *Esther! Come on! You've slept enough! Help me with the chores! Light the stove!* It felt strange not having her around to tell me what to do. Everything was so peaceful—but a little lonely too.

I stepped out of the bedroom in my bare feet and felt the smooth floor tiles. The bedroom opened right to the kitchen. Eggs had been piled into a bowl, and a slab of butter, a loaf of bread, and a bottle of milk were neatly arranged on the kitchen table. Just beyond was the yard. It was blooming with flowers that looked too beautiful to be real. I saw a washstand and a clothesline, from which hung Papa's shirt and pants, the thick dress I had worn on the ship, and the wool stockings that I hoped to never wear again. I had slept so soundly I had not woken up before Papa to do the laundry myself.

I went back inside and walked through the kitchen into the front room. I found a familiar and comforting sight—Papa, his eyes half-closed, bobbed back and forth, praying in the Cuban dawn. I stood watching, not daring to interrupt. Only when he finished did he open his eyes and notice I was there.

"My daughter," he said. "You are here."

Tears came to his eyes and to mine.

"My prayers did some good. Now let's see if the two of us can get the rest of our family out of Poland. I won't be at peace until we're all together again."

I told Papa I wouldn't be either, and then I got ready for the day. There's an outhouse and next to it a washroom where you can throw a bucket of water over yourself and get clean. The cool water felt good on my sweaty skin. My dress on the clothesline had dried, so I put it on and rinsed out my other one—but by the time I was finished, I was hot all over again in my wool dress.

I made breakfast, boiling the eggs, warming the milk on the charcoal stove, and slicing the bread. It was nice to work slowly, at my own pace, without Mama looking over my shoulder. Was I doing it all correctly? I didn't know. But I felt grown-up and free. Then Papa showed me how to make coffee, which filled the house with a pleasant smell, like wet earth. He said I could add a few spoonfuls to my milk and pointed to a tin can filled to the brim with brown sugar. Can you believe I was allowed to take all I wanted, Malka? Sugar is plentiful in Cuba. I took a whole spoonful and let it melt in my mouth. It tasted like happiness.

Papa smiled his sad smile. "There were many days after I first arrived that I made do with sugar and water."

I told Papa, "If that's all there is to eat, I can make do on sugar and water too."

"No, my child, I will not allow that to happen to you," Papa said.

He took my hand and we went to the front room, where there are two rocking chairs and the cot where Papa sleeps now that I have the only bedroom in the house. We sat side by side. Never having sat in a rocking chair before, I held on to the armrests, worrying about tipping over. Papa laughed and said I should enjoy its movement. He rocked back and forth playfully to show me the chair was designed to move this way, and then I laughed too. Papa said that people in Cuba love rocking chairs and sit in them for hours, talking and telling stories.

We rested for most of the day because it was Shabbos. Then the next day, I asked Papa if I could see what we would be selling, and he lowered his head as if ashamed. He picked up the satchel and pulled out plaster figurines painted in bright colors. "This is what I sell. Please don't judge me too harshly."

I looked at the small statues. There was a Jesus Child and a Mother Mary in a yellow gown and a Mother Mary in a blue gown. And there were saints I didn't recognize, painted in red, in purple, and in green.

"Oh, my daughter. Forgive me. Hopefully our God will forgive me too."

"Papa, I forgive you. This is what you had to do to survive in Cuba, and our God understands and forgives. We will sell the idols so we can save money and bring the family to Cuba. One day you will have a store here like you had in Poland."

"You're a dreamer, Esther. But let's go and give it a try. It's Sunday and maybe people will be in a generous mood. Those who went to church will be ready to do a good deed, and those who stayed home will perhaps want to help a wandering father and daughter."

We organized the small statues, placing all the same kinds and same sizes together. I told Papa to give me some to carry in another satchel, and we set off.

I ask you, dear Malka, please do not *ever* tell Mama about the idols that Papa has sold in Cuba. I fear she'd react with anger and have no sympathy for Papa.

Your sister, who loves you,

Esther

AGRAMONTE

February 7, 1938

Dearest sister Malka,

So yesterday, Papa and I set off with our satchels and had only taken a few steps when someone called out, "Mira, el polaco, con una polaquita." That is how they addressed us: "Look, the Polish man, with a little Polish girl." Soon a group of people gathered around us to get a good look at me.

Papa told them, "Mi hija," my daughter.

"Niña linda," they said. Pretty girl. And they kissed my cheeks as if they'd known me all my life. I thought it was just the lady selling fruit in Havana who was friendly, but the people in Agramonte are so friendly too.

We walked along the main road of the town, Calle Independencia, passing a pharmacy, a hardware store, a general store, and a hat store. The stores have tall columns in front with awnings that give shade to the sidewalk. The owners sit inside fanning themselves. They're not peddlers like us who have to go find customers.

It was still early and the air smelled like candy from the nearby sugar mills. We made our way to the edge of town along a dirt path. Bees were buzzing and the squawks of cows, goats, and pigs filled our ears. Men rode past on horses, nodding hello. I tiptoed through the muddy streets in my new sandals, then finally gave up on trying to keep my feet clean. Papa said that with the humidity and the rain in Cuba, the streets are almost always muddy, so I might as well get used to it.

We came to an area full of little wooden houses with palm-thatched roofs. Most of the doors were open, and the people sitting outside waved as we passed and said, "Buenos días," which means "Good morning." We waved and said "Buenos días" in return. Now and then, someone called out, "Polaco, ¿cómo le va?" meaning "Polish man, how are you?" Although they don't all know Papa, they know from his looks that he's a Jewish peddler.

Papa told me to keep walking and if anyone asked to see what we were selling, we'd stop and show them the merchandise. I thought we'd never sell anything that way, but it wasn't long before an older woman called out to us. We stopped and Papa pulled out a few statues. The woman smiled and invited us into her home. She pointed to the sun and pressed her hand to her forehead to signal it was too hot to stay outside.

Inside, she motioned us to sit down in some rocking chairs as she took a seat on a stool and spread her blue-and-white skirt around her like flower petals. Her hair was wrapped inside a matching blue-and-white scarf.

She pointed to our bags, and when we took out all the

statues, she didn't hesitate. She chose a medium-sized statue of the Virgin Mary dressed in a long white dress and a blue cape and holding a pale baby in her arms. The skin of this Mary was as black as hers.

Papa looked at the statue and said, "Virgen María."

But the woman shook her head and replied, "Yemayá."

Papa looked confused.

The woman stood and again motioned to us, this time asking us to follow her through a door into another room. "Look, there is Yemayá," she said, pointing to a fountain of water sprouting from the ground.

The woman bent down and I did too. "Agua," she said. Papa told me that was the word for water in Spanish.

"Agua," I repeated, and she smiled and repeated "Yemayá" so we understood that the water, the fountain, and Yemayá were all connected.

She told Papa she wanted to buy the statue but could only pay half the amount. Papa told her that if that was all she could pay, it was fine. I imagined how upset Mama would be to hear him—she would say that Papa is the worst salesman. But I wish you all could have seen how the woman's eyes lit up and with what affection she hugged Papa, practically lifting him off his feet. Then she took the statue and carefully placed it on the ground next to the fountain.

We packed up the rest of our things and were about to leave when a young girl and a handsome man appeared carrying baskets filled with pineapples and bananas. They had black skin but not as dark as the woman's. "Buenos días," they said.

I couldn't understand what the woman told them, but I made out the words "polacos" and "Yemayá," enough to know she was explaining to them that she'd gotten the statue from us for half its cost. The woman had barely finished speaking when the man reached into one of the baskets and pulled out a pineapple. He passed it to me and said, "Dulce."

As best I could, I replied, "Gracias."

The girl smiled at me. We were the same height and I figured we were about the same age. I pointed to myself and said, "Esther," and she pointed to herself and said, "Manuela." Then she pointed to the woman and said, "Abuela," which Papa whispered meant grandmother, and she added "Ma Felipa" to let me know that was her name. Pointing to the man, she said, "Papá." And she told me her father's name was Mario José.

We left and wandered the backcountry roads for hours in the hot sun, hoping to make a few sales. Papa pointed to an old stone building that was so long it seemed to stretch for miles and miles. He said that's where the people who work on the sugarcane plantations live, lots of different families all crowded together. Some of the workers were sitting outside and nodded politely to us, while others looked too tired to even smile. No one asked to see what we carried in our satchels.

I was glad we at least had a pineapple to show for our efforts. When we got home, Papa peeled and cut it, and we enjoyed the delicious fruit. Then Papa put the money we earned from our one humble sale in a box under my bed. We'll need to sell more in the days to come, because at this rate it will take forever to get you here, little sister, and I can't wait that long.

With my love as always,
ESTHER

AGRAMONTE

February 15, 1938

Dear Malka,

I was waiting to write until I could share some cheerful news. This past week started badly, but it ended up so much better!

For days and days, Papa and I could find no more customers. Not only is Papa shy about displaying our statues, but he'll hardly speak to anybody. I think it's because he has no confidence in the little bit of Spanish he's learned.

At the end of the week, I decided it was time to meet our neighbors on Calle Independencia. Papa warned me not to try selling near the stores. He said the shopkeepers would become angry and think we were trying to take away their business.

While Papa was saying his morning prayers, I headed outside with my satchel and walked past the stores, waving hello. To anyone in sight, I said, "Buenos días." After that I didn't know what to say and I didn't understand anything of what they said to me, except that they all called me "la polaquita."

The door to the grocery store was open. The Chinese owner

stood behind the counter and nodded to me as I came in. Next to him was a Chinese boy who looked to be about my age.

I pointed to myself and said, "Esther."

The old man pointed to himself and said, "Juan Chang," and then the boy pointed to himself and said, "Francisco Chang."

Behind the counter were shelves filled with things for sale. Glass jars held interesting-looking sauces, and bottles of oil and vinegar and tins of tea gleamed in the sun streaming through the open door. Pictures of cows decorated cans of condensed milk, and pictures of fish decorated cans of anchovies and mackerel.

I don't know why, but I had a feeling they wouldn't mind if I showed them what I had for sale—and I was right! Juan Chang smiled as I took the statues out, and he and Francisco made space so I could line them up on the counter.

When I pulled out the male figure wearing a purple cape, with wounds on his legs and a dog on either side of him, they exclaimed, "¡San Lázaro! Li Xuan!" Francisco wrote out the Spanish and Chinese names for me on a piece of paper so I could understand it was Saint Lazarus.

They called the figure in the blue gown—the one that Ma Felipa, the woman with the fountain in her house, called Yemayá—the Virgen de Regla. I remembered seeing the Virgin of Regla's shrine when the ship sailed into Havana and the sailors thanked her for our safe voyage. It was all starting to make sense—Regla and Yemayá were one and the same and connected to the water. They told me her Chinese name, which is Ama, meant "abuela." I felt so proud that I already knew that was the word for grandmother.

Then Juan Chang surprised me by reaching into a metal box and pulling out enough money to buy five statues!

"Gracias," I said, not knowing many other words in Spanish. And I ran all the way back to our house, eager to tell Papa how well I had done.

"Esther, I hope you sold the religious items honestly," he said.

"Of course I did, Papa!"

He replied, "My child, then you have done better in one morning than I in all the years I've been here."

We had enough to buy a chicken, which Papa slaughtered in the kosher way, making sure we didn't eat any of its blood, since the blood is the life force of all living things and we have no right to take that away from any creature. Papa said a prayer of thanks, and we roasted the chicken and ate it happily, putting away the rest of our earnings in the savings box under my bed.

Your loving sister,

ESTHER

AGRAMONTE

February 18, 1938

Dear Malka,

Ever since Papa has allowed me to show the merchandise to people, we've been selling the Christian statues easily around town.

I think Cubans are amused by me. "Look at what the little Polish girl is selling," they say. I must look silly in my woolen dresses, but until I can make myself a lighter dress, I'll have to make do. I don't mind making them chuckle if it will help bring you all here sooner.

Today we crossed paths with a most elegant woman. She was pale and dressed completely in black. She greeted Papa, "¿Cómo está, Señor Abraham?"

He nodded politely and said, "Muy bien, Señora Graciela."

The woman looked at me and asked, "¿Su hija?"

Again he nodded.

"Por favor," she said, and pointed to a pretty house on the corner with tall columns and balconies edged with wrought-iron railings.

Papa whispered to me, "That's Señora Graciela, the doctor's

wife. She's renting us the house we're living in for very little money. We'll visit for a moment."

Señora Graciela's house smelled of lilac perfume and had high ceilings and a piano. The paintings on the walls were of landscapes—hills with tall palm trees, fields of sugarcane, and waves crashing against the seashore. And then there was one large painting of a girl in a ruffled dress, with pale skin and golden amber eyes, like Señora Graciela's.

Señora Graciela motioned for us to sit down and left the room. She came back with her husband, Doctor Pablo. He has thick hair that is completely gray, even though he looks years younger than Papa. His dark eyes shone above his glasses, which he wears on the tip of his nose. He and Papa shook hands. Then Doctor Pablo turned to me and said, "Buenos días, Esther." Papa must have told him my name. I was glad not to be called "la polaquita" for once.

I said "Gracias" instead of "Buenos días."

Doctor Pablo laughed. He said a few words to Señora Graciela, and she said a few words to Papa.

They wanted us to have dinner with them, and I knew this would worry Papa since the food wouldn't be kosher and we'd break a commandment of our religion by eating it. But he couldn't turn down the doctor and his wife. Whatever they served for dinner, even if it was pork, we'd eat it. Then we'd rinse out our mouths and Papa would say prayers and ask to be forgiven.

We went back to the house to wash up and change into our

clean set of clothes, and when we returned, the table was set with plates trimmed in gold. The forks and knives and spoons were made of real silver and the glasses were made of crystal. I was afraid to touch anything for fear of breaking it, and I'm sure Papa felt the same!

Señora Graciela brought out the first dish, which was a tomato soup. I lifted my heavy spoon and dipped it into the bowl. The soup was cold! Doctor Pablo and Señora Graciela acted as if nothing was wrong. How could a soup be cold? I knew what Mama would say: *If a soup doesn't burn your mouth, it isn't a soup.* Papa and I ate without saying a word.

Señora Graciela brought out one dish after another. We ate potatoes that tasted sweet and were called "boniato." Bananas cooked in oil that also tasted sweet were called "plátano frito." There were black beans, or "frijoles negros," and something soft and green that melted in your mouth, which they called "aguacate," or avocado. I kept expecting the meat to appear, the pork we'd swallow against our will, but Señora Graciela brought out nothing more.

Señora Graciela looked over at Papa and said something that made Papa smile for a moment, but then he became sad.

"Tell me, Papa," I whispered.

Señora Graciela nodded to Papa, giving him permission to translate what she'd said.

Then Papa turned to me and explained, "She has only served us vegetables for dinner because Doctor Pablo is a vegetarian."

I looked back at Papa and asked, "Is that all she told you? Why did you become sad?"

He sighed. Then he said, "They had a daughter around your age named Emilia—a name that starts with an *E*, just like yours. She died a year ago from leukemia. To be a doctor and not be able to save his daughter broke Doctor Pablo's heart, and so he eats only vegetables as penance and skips the stewed meat and roasted pork that most Cubans adore."

Señora Graciela wiped tears from her eyes and Doctor Pablo clasped her hand. I wished I could say some consoling words in Spanish.

Before we left, Señora Graciela told us the girl in the painting was Emilia, and she gave me a Spanish grammar book that had belonged to her daughter. Her name was neatly written on the front page. I felt terrible that this girl had died so young and left her mother and father so sad.

I imagined Emilia smiling down at me as I stayed up all night studying the lessons in her Spanish grammar book, pronouncing aloud the verbs and nouns as I lay in bed. I fell asleep with Spanish words on my tongue, words that are starting to feel more and more familiar.

With all my love as always,

Esther

AGRAMONTE

February 22, 1938

Dear Malka,

I am sorry to have to tell you that yesterday we had our first ugly experience in Cuba. With only a few statues left to sell, and not wanting to bother the people who had already bought from us, Papa and I set off to the neighborhood where Ma Felipa, the woman with the indoor fountain, lives. We were a few feet from her door when a man in a straw hat riding a tall brown horse came galloping our way. We moved aside as fast as we could, afraid he'd trample us.

"¡Fuera, judíos!" he yelled.

I knew right away that "judíos" meant Jews.

He dismounted and grabbed my satchel, pulling out a Saint Lazarus statue. Then he tore Papa's satchel from his shoulder, shouted "¡Judíos!" again, and gave Papa a shove.

Just then we heard a woman's scream, "¡No!" Her voice pierced the air and the man froze. It was Ma Felipa, dressed in her blue-and-white skirt with the blue-and-white scarf wrapped around her head. Manuela, her granddaughter, stood next to her. I understood enough Spanish to know Ma Felipa was telling the man to leave. He listened to her respectfully but then spat on the ground by Papa's feet, got back on his horse, and galloped away.

Papa was trembling and I was too. I took his hand and tried to steady him. Manuela picked up the satchels from the ground and Ma Felipa led us into her house. We sank down into her rocking chairs and I continued to hold Papa's hand. Ma Felipa left and came back with two glasses of water for us.

"Yemayá," she said.

It was the water from the fountain in her house, and it tasted cool and refreshing.

After we drank the water, Manuela and Ma Felipa stood before us, rocking back and forth and singing in a language I'd never heard before.

Yemayá Asesu
Asesu Yemayá
Yemayá Olodo
Olodo Yemayá . . .

They repeated the words so many times, I still remember them. The tune was so beautiful I can't get it out of my head. I have been singing the song to myself ever since.

When we got up to leave, they helped us lift our satchels back onto our shoulders. Mario José arrived with a basket of fruit, and after Manuela and Ma Felipa told him what happened, he insisted on giving us another pineapple.

Cubans have been so friendly to me that I almost forgot

about how some people hate Jews. I am worried that if the hatred toward Jews has reached all the way across the ocean to Cuba, things must be getting much worse in Poland. I hope that you and the family are safe, Malka. If only I could speak to you for even a minute! But the distance between us is as wide as the sea. Now I am even more determined to work hard to bring you all here.

With all my love,
ESTHER

AGRAMONTE

February 25, 1938

Dear Malka,

Yesterday morning, we stepped out of the house with our satchels on our shoulders, ready to try to sell the last of our statues, but we didn't get very far. There he was—the man on the horse! Papa clasped my hand and said we should go back inside. But it was too late. The man saw us and glared at us but fortunately left us alone. He tied his horse to a post and knocked on the door of Doctor Pablo and Señora Graciela. We watched as he went inside. We thought we'd scramble down the street before he came out, but a moment later, we were face-to-face with him. Papa and I, both short and small, trembled at the sight of him. With his long legs and big boots, he was a giant.

But Señora Graciela came to his side, and in her friendly way, she said to us, "Señor Abraham and Esther! Let me introduce you to my brother."

So that man with the horse was her brother! How could such a kind woman be related to such a cruel man? "This is Señor Eduardo," she went on, telling him we were "polacos" who had just moved into town.

He sneered and said, "They're not polacos, they're judíos." To him, we are nothing but Jews.

He raised one of his long legs into the air to climb onto his horse, and galloped away, stirring up a cloud of dust that got caught in our throats. Señora Graciela blew away the dust from her face with a fan she expertly snapped open, then insisted we come to her house.

Doctor Pablo greeted us warmly, patting Papa on the back and hugging me, and urged us to sit in the living room with him and Señora Graciela under the portrait of Emilia.

Señora Graciela told Doctor Pablo about our encounter with her brother. The doctor shook his head and looked at us with sad eyes. "Lo siento, lo siento," he said, which Papa told me meant he was sorry. Doctor Pablo said many other things I didn't understand, but I caught several words. Papa explained everything to me later while we rested in our rocking chairs before going to sleep.

Papa said there is a terrible war going on in Spain, and Doctor Pablo and Señor Eduardo are on opposite sides. Both their grandfathers came from Spain to Cuba. Doctor Pablo is a Republicano who believes all religions should be respected and Cuba should be a place where immigrants can work and progress. Señor Eduardo does not agree. He is a Falangista who wants everyone in Cuba to be of the Catholic faith, like in Spain.

Señor Eduardo is the owner of a sugar mill near Agramonte that has been in his and Señora Graciela's family for many generations. Almost all the black people in Agramonte work in their sugar mill. Many white people who've arrived penniless from Spain in the last few years also work there.

"I've been told there are still a few elders left here who were once enslaved," Papa said. "They were brought to Cuba from Africa to work cutting cane and making sugar in the mills."

"They must have suffered so much," I said.

Papa nodded. "Yes, they did. The slave owners were very cruel to the African people here. They kept them in chains so they wouldn't run away."

I was shocked. I thought slavery had ended long ago. "How can anybody own somebody?" I asked.

Papa replied, "The slave masters owned their bodies. But they found out they couldn't own their souls."

It was late, and the sound of crickets chirping and palm trees rustling in the breeze filled the room.

Papa said, "Now let's get some rest."

I had more questions, but Papa was falling asleep in his chair.

"Papa, do you think Ma Felipa was enslaved once?"

He stood up slowly. "I don't know. Maybe one day she will tell us her story."

I went to sleep humming Ma Felipa's song about the saint of the sea—Yemayá Asesu, Asesu Yemayá—and wondering if it came from Africa.

With all the love a sister can give,
ESTHER

AGRAMONTE

March 1, 1938

Dear Malka,

I think Señora Graciela invited us to dinner again so soon because she felt bad about the way her brother, Señor Eduardo, treated us. Tonight we had another delicious vegetarian meal. This time we began with "frituras de maíz," corn cakes that were really good; you would've loved them! Then she brought out a huge platter of "arroz frito," which is fried rice. It had peas and carrots and little squares of scrambled eggs. What made it so tasty was the "salsa china," a Chinese sauce she told us she gets from the store owned by Juan Chang.

"He sells things from all over the world!" Señora Graciela exclaimed.

I smiled, thinking of how kind he'd been to me.

Papa asked if Juan Chang had been in Agramonte a long time, and she said he arrived ten years ago. He was Cantonese and came by himself to Cuba. He married a black woman and it was a happy marriage, but she and their baby died in childbirth. Such a sad story, Señora Graciela said. His store was all he lived for. But he was lonely. He sent for his nephew, Francisco Chang, who came from China to live and work with him.

Dinner ended and Señora Graciela turned to Papa and said she wanted to buy all the religious statues we still had left for sale.

Papa said there was no reason for her to do such a thing. But Doctor Pablo explained that Señora Graciela was a devout Catholic and would appreciate having the Virgin and the saints on her nightstand, where she could light a candle and pray to them before going to sleep, so they might take care of their beloved daughter, Emilia, whom they had lost too young.

I imagined Emilia was now a star shining from the light of her mother's candles and prayers.

On our way out, Señora Graciela gave me another book that had belonged to Emilia, a book of poems by José Martí. She said it was called *Simple Verses* and I could read and enjoy the poems to help me learn Spanish. I remembered the statue of José Martí in the Parque Central in Havana and how Papa had said never to say a bad word about José Martí because he is so respected by Cubans.

Later that night, I fell asleep reciting the lines "Yo vengo de todas partes / Y hacia todas partes voy."

The words are simple, but they mean so much: "I come from many places / And to every place I go." That is how I feel now, Malka. I'm in a place that wasn't mine but is slowly feeling like it could become my home.

This morning, we brought Señora Graciela all the idols we had left—including a large figurine of the Virgin of Regla, or Yemayá, as Ma Felipa and Manuela call her. Many people had admired this statue. It was beautiful, but very heavy, and I had felt bad seeing Papa weighed down as he carried it from road to road. I was glad it would be in Señora Graciela's possession and help her send love to Emilia, whom she misses and mourns every day in her black clothes.

I am certain Señora Graciela and Doctor Pablo bought the idols from us not only so she could pray to them, but also because they don't want us to be insulted again by Señor Eduardo.

Now that we don't have any more statues to sell, Papa and I must go to Havana tomorrow. Papa needs to pay Zvi Mandelbaum a commission on what we have sold. Then we can start fresh with new things to sell. All I want is to keep saving up for our family's journey here.

How I miss you, dear Malka. I remember you would bring home books from the library and stay up reading all night. I imagine you studying and getting smarter every day. Books are precious, aren't they? I can't imagine how we'd live without them. They're powerful too—I guess that's why there are people in this world who hate books so much that they burn them. Would you believe that happened in Germany a few years ago? It scares me to think it could happen again. Hopefully it will not be long before you are in Cuba and staying up reading the verses of José Martí.

With all my love as always,
ESTHER

AGRAMONTE

March 2, 1938

Dear Malka,

I wish you could have seen the look of surprise on Zvi Mandelbaum's face when he learned we had sold everything that he'd given to Papa to peddle.

"Avrum, you never sell out so fast. Esther has brought you good luck!"

"Yes, she has, Zvi," Papa replied, smiling at me.

"So let me give you more of the idols to sell," Zvi said.

Papa shook his head. "Give us something else to sell."

Zvi reached into a box filled with sandals like the ones he had given me and said, "How about sandals? Everyone needs sandals! You see people running around barefoot in the countryside, hurting their feet. Offer them sandals and they will be grateful, you will see."

He told Papa he would take only a small commission if we sold them quickly. We walked out with our satchels full, Papa with sandals for men and boys and I with sandals for women and girls.

We walked along Calle Muralla, peeking at the window displays of the fabric shops owned by Jewish immigrants. There were bolts of cloth in every color and pattern you can imagine. I thought of Mama and what an artist she is with needle and thread. She taught me to sew—not with a lot of patience—but what does that matter now? Do you remember, Malka, how when we were little, I made patchwork skirts for our dolls out of scraps of cloth? That seems so long ago.

I asked Papa if we could buy fabric, scissors, needles, and thread so I could make some dresses. After sweating in my wool dress for a month, I was eager to change into something soft and light. Papa agreed, and we picked a store and went inside.

The kind woman who helped us is also from Poland. Her name is Rifka Rubenstein and she speaks Yiddish in the same singsong way as Bubbe. It almost brought tears to my eyes to hear her.

For a few pennies, we bought yards of remnants in several colors. I made sure to get cloth in a nice shade of blue, thinking of a dress I could make for Ma Felipa. I even chose a bit of black fabric to make a dress for Señora Graciela. There were two pretty floral prints in a light cotton as smooth as butter, and I took those too, thinking they'd be nice for dresses for Manuela and for me. I got scissors, needles, pins, and thread. And I remembered to get a tape measure, the kind that rolls up and fits in my pocket, and some tracing paper and pencils to be able to draw the patterns.

I was so excited by all my purchases, I kissed the woman goodbye as we were leaving.

That brought a tear to her eye. She said I reminded her of a granddaughter she had left behind in Poland. Then she reached behind the counter where she was sitting and pulled out a big box of buttons, all shapes and sizes, and gave them to me. She told me to return whenever I needed more supplies, and she would always give me a good price.

We were hungry by then, so we stopped at La Flor de Berlín and bought two challahs, one to devour as we walked around Havana and the other to bring back with us to Agramonte. Of course, Papa and I said the prayer first before we dug in. We were both so hungry! But how strange it felt to be eating that braided bread that reminded me of you and Mama and Bubbe and my brothers and my old life in Poland while the sun shone bright, the sea air gave off a scent of faraway places, and street vendors roamed the humid streets selling peanuts and fruit ices. It was all Papa and I needed for lunch. We were eager to return to Agramonte and start selling the sandals. I wanted to sit and sew and see what dresses I could make on my own, without Mama looking over my shoulder.

But Papa felt he had to go to synagogue, if only for a few minutes, to pray with other men and remember he wasn't alone in the wilderness. We stopped in for afternoon prayers, and Papa sat with the men while I sat on the women's side.

There was only one woman sitting there with a girl who seemed a bit older than me. We were too far from the men to hear the prayers, so I whispered to the woman in Yiddish, asking if they had been in Cuba for very long.

"My daughter and I just arrived," she responded. She spoke Yiddish with a different accent than I was used to, but we could understand each other. "We are from Germany," she said. She wiped away a tear. "Things are getting very bad there for the Jews."

Her daughter put her arm around her mother to comfort her. "We were fortunate to be able to escape. Papa is safe in Bolivia and we'll be reunited soon."

Her mother shivered, even though it was hot in the synagogue. "There is a terrible man in power in Germany. His name is Hitler. He hates Jews and Romani people and sick people—and anyone who disagrees with him. His followers, the Nazis, took everything from us—not just our home, but our hopes and dreams."

"We will find new hopes and dreams here, and we will begin again," the girl said. She held her mother even tighter. I realized at that moment how much I wanted to hug Bubbe and Mama, and you, dear Malka, and even my brothers if they'd let me!

Hearing about the Jewish people in Germany got me even more worried about what might be happening to all of you in Poland. Not knowing if you're hungry, if the dark winter days are filled with fear, I feel an ache in my heart. But even if I could look into a magic glass and see all of you, there's little I can do from this great distance, and that hurts more. I know Papa feels helpless and desperate whenever he receives a letter from Mama. He doesn't let me read these letters, which come so rarely and arrive so ragged they look as if they're filled with clumps of sadness.

When the prayers ended at the synagogue, I said goodbye to the mother and daughter and wished them well. Papa and I found our way to the train station, carrying our satchels stuffed with sandals and the sewing things, but what really weighed heavily on us were our worries for the future.

With love from your sister,
ESTHER

AGRAMONTE

March 7, 1938

Dearest Malka,

I've spent the last few days making a dress for myself, sewing early in the morning when the light is bright, while Papa prays. I sketched the pattern on tracing paper and then chose one of the floral cotton fabrics, placed it on the pattern, and cut the material. I decided on a simple collar and short capped sleeves. I began to sew, following the picture in my imagination. I thought it should button up the front to make it easy to take on and off. I tucked in the waist a bit so it would fit nicely.

I basted first, using big stitches to hold the pieces together and be sure it looked like a real dress. We only have a small mirror that Papa uses to shave. When I tried the dress on, it was difficult to see how it fit, but I caught enough of a glimpse to think I'd done pretty well. I twirled around and the fabric felt like a cool breeze as it swept past my legs.

Confident it looked good, I sat down and stitched it all together with small, tight stitches so the dress would hold up to lots of wear and washings. Mama's silver thimble came in handy! For the final touch, I added pockets at the hips, where they'd be easy to use and I could easily find my pocket watch. I love pockets and won't make any dresses without them!

When Papa saw the dress, he was impressed! "Beautiful sewing, Esther," he said. "Your mother's lessons weren't in vain."

I thought of Mama and was surprised at how much I missed her . . . Now that we're apart, I wish we hadn't argued so much and had been more patient with each other. But I know for sure she'd be proud of this dress!

Feeling light as a feather in my cotton dress, I went off with Papa to sell sandals. Zvi Mandelbaum was right about people in the countryside needing them. So many are barefoot or wearing torn-up shoes. Papa decided to sell the sandals for less than Zvi Mandelbaum suggested so even the sugarcane workers living out of town in the barracks could afford them. He lets people pay half now and the rest in a month if they can't afford the full cost. Papa says this is called an installment plan and it's a new thing.

Everyone is happy with this arrangement because they get to wear the sandals right away. Papa asked me to keep a record of all the loans, and this way I am learning the names of our neighbors in Agramonte and in the hamlets near the sugar mill.

Now when the people there see us coming down the road, they're friendly and take us inside their houses so they can try them on.

Ma Felipa also heard about the sandals we were selling. On our way back home, she called to us and said she wanted to buy sandals for Manuela. Papa refused to take any money from her. We would be forever grateful that she saved us from the cruelty of Señor Eduardo. If not for her, who knows what he might have done to Papa?

"It's a gift," Papa said. "Un regalo" in Spanish.

Ma Felipa was so touched, she gave Papa one of her big hugs. Manuela was giddy in her new sandals, which are just like mine, but the leather's still clean and shiny. She danced around and then extended her hand to me so we danced together. When she said, "Amigas!" I felt so happy. I've been wanting to make a friend here in Cuba, someone my age to spend time with. I will put even more effort into learning Spanish if I have a friend, though I have learned a lot already, as I mostly understand what I hear and have learned to count to one hundred.

Manuela helps her family with their work too. She helps Mario José in the fields, and she helps Ma Felipa around the house with the cooking and cleaning and feeding the chickens they keep in the yard. She finished elementary school in Agramonte, but there is no secondary school in the town.

Manuela rubbed the skin on her arm with her finger and used this gesture to show that her skin is a different color from mine. She said, "Most black people here were not taught how to read and write until recently." Then she pointed to Ma Felipa and said, "Fue esclava," meaning "She was enslaved."

It was what I had imagined, and I felt sad to know it was true. Ma Felipa nodded and placed her wrists against each other and brought both arms up to her heart, showing how she had once been in chains. Manuela said Ma Felipa wasn't allowed to learn to read or write, but she had taught her grandmother to write her name and is slowly teaching her the alphabet. Manuela says she dreams of being a schoolteacher, "una maestra," one day, and teaching in their elementary school. She wants to see the grandchildren and great-grandchildren of people who were once enslaved learn how to read and write. I was so impressed hearing her speak, and I hope her dream will come true.

"Ven conmigo," Manuela said, and led me outdoors to the field behind their house while Papa and Ma Felipa remained indoors, resting in the rocking chairs.

We walked a few feet and stopped before a tree.

"Ceiba," she said.

It was a tall tree with a few limbs and a canopy of rustling leaves. Rather than being underground, the roots bulged from the earth, thick and strong. Manuela showed me a chain wrapped around the trunk of the ceiba. Candles and flowers had been left at the base of the tree as offerings. The chain had belonged to a slave, Manuela said. The tree held the suffering of all the slaves who asked for help, and sometimes at night, when the suffering becomes too much for it, tears drip down the trunk. She pantomimed that she was crying to make sure I understood the meaning of the word "lágrimas."

I had never heard of a tree that could cry, but so many things are different in Cuba.

We went back inside and Papa said it was time to go. I

remembered I wanted to take their measurements so I could make dresses for Ma Felipa and Manuela. I was clumsy trying to explain what I wanted. But then I pointed to my dress and they both said, "Un vestido." They were delighted once they understood I had sewn the dress myself. They let me measure them with my tape and I wrote the numbers down in the back of Papa's ledger, then we picked up our satchels and said goodbye.

At the door I turned, and Manuela looked back and said to me, "Amigas."

I repeated, "Amigas."

The very next morning, I promised myself, I had to begin sewing a dress for Manuela, my first friend in Cuba.

My dear Malka, I will tell you more in the next letter. I'm so tired I'm falling asleep as I write. The only thing keeping me awake is the sound of crickets singing in the night, and the desire to write everything down for you so I don't forget any details. I don't know if you're awake or sleeping now, but I hope you are well in every way, as I love you with all my heart.

Wishing you good
dreams always,
Esther

AGRAMONTE

March 10, 1938

My dear Malka,

For the last three days, I got up early and sewed and sewed until I finished the dress for Manuela. I was able to sew faster because I knew what I was doing and Manuela and I are the same size. I also made hers with buttons in the front, but I experimented and tucked the pockets into the seams so they're hidden.

"Can I go over to Manuela's house and give her the dress?" I asked Papa after he was done praying. Papa agreed and said he was going to do some accounting and see how much we had earned from the sale of the sandals.

No sooner had I gotten beyond the town center and was walking on the dirt path that led to Manuela's house than Señor Eduardo appeared on his horse. I kept my gaze down and moved to the edge of the path, trying to make myself invisible, but he turned his horse around and followed me. He didn't say a word, but I could feel the heat of his horse's breath on my back. Then when I got to the door of Ma Felipa's house, he muttered "judía" and sped away.

Manuela greeted me with a hug and waved me into the house. I tried not to give Señor Eduardo any more thought as I followed her inside.

"Tengo un regalo," I said. I have a gift.

I gave her the folded bundle. She opened it and was thrilled to find the dress. She kept turning it from front to back, looking at every seam and every detail, admiring the yellow buttons I'd chosen to match the flowers on the dress, and saying "bonito," which means "beautiful." Ma Felipa came into the room and she marveled at the dress too. When Manuela tried it on, I was happy to see the dress fit perfectly. She twirled around as I had and I could tell she enjoyed the breezy feeling of the light cotton fabric on her legs too. This dress was even lighter than the simple shift she usually wore, made out of muslin. "Gracias," she said, and gave me a hug, and then Ma Felipa gave me a hug. Next I'll surprise Ma Felipa with a dress—I already know what design I'll make for her.

Ma Felipa wouldn't let me leave without giving me a cluster of bananas. As soon as I went out the door, I checked to be sure Señor Eduardo was nowhere in sight and rushed all the way back home.

I was glad to find Papa in a cheerful mood. He added up our sales and said our savings under the bed were growing. Soon he'll send money to Mama for food and put aside money for the steamship tickets for all of you.

We went out to sell sandals in the afternoon and I tried not to worry about Señor Eduardo appearing out of nowhere.

I wondered if I'd imagined it all. I hoped I had. I wish you could tell me, dear Malka, that I imagined it—didn't I?

With all my love
and still more love,
Esther

AGRAMONTE

March 14, 1938

Dear Malka,

I am getting better and better at sewing. But it's true I spent all of Saturday night and Sunday doing little else. For the dress for Ma Felipa, I used the blue fabric and designed it to be looser and longer so it would be comfortable and flow like the water of her Yemayá fountain. I added iridescent mother-of-pearl buttons down the front and cut a big square of fabric she can use as a kerchief.

Papa came with me to deliver the dress and kerchief to Ma Felipa. When I gave the things to her, she began to sing, "Yemayá, Yemayá," and sprinkled water from the fountain onto the dress. Then she went to the other room and changed into the dress and tied the kerchief around her head. Upon returning, she stretched out her arms and hugged Papa and me at the same time and said, "Bendiciones," which Papa told me means "blessings."

The next dress I decided to make was a black one for Señora Graciela. I knew I couldn't make anything as elegant as the dresses she wore every day, but I designed it with a high collar and a bow at the top of the neck and gathered it at the waist with a full skirt. I also made hidden pockets for her dress. Señora Graciela can use them for her many handkerchiefs. I borrowed the measurements for Ma Felipa's dress since the two women are about the same size. The only difference is Ma Felipa is taller, so I made Señora Graciela's dress a bit shorter.

Señora Graciela was astonished I had made the dress myself. She ran to her bedroom to try it on and returned in a rush of excitement about how well it fit. She was stunned I had crafted it with the hidden pockets and instinctively placed the two handkerchiefs she was carrying inside them. She called in Doctor Pablo to see my handiwork. They marveled at my "gran talento."

"¿Te gusta coser?" Señora Graciela asked me.

She asked if I liked to sew. I now understood those words in Spanish!

I responded, "Sí, me gusta." I've learned that I actually do like to sew.

"Muy bien," Señora Graciela said, pleased by my response. Then she asked if I wanted a máquina de coser.

A sewing machine? Of course I wanted a sewing machine! I thought about all the dresses I could make in a week if I didn't have to stitch them together by hand.

Señora Graciela said she had an old sewing machine that belonged to an aunt who moved to el norte. Pulling a handkerchief out of the pocket of the dress I'd sewn, Señora Graciela dried a tear and explained how she had dreamed of making dresses for Emilia, but could neither cut nor sew straight. Doctor Pablo put an arm around Señora Graciela's shoulders, and I thought how fortunate she was to be married to a doctor who could care for her, although no doctor could heal her sorrow.

Then a smile appeared on Señora Graciela's face. She said she had never imagined a sweet girl like me would come along—a girl who could sew her own clothes. That I was like a gift from the sky, "del cielo," she said. If I would accept her gift of the sewing machine, she would feel so happy.

I turned to Papa, not knowing if I could accept such an enormous gift. Now I was excited about the idea of making lots of dresses and selling them. I hadn't thought of that when I started sewing; I just wanted to get out of my itchy wool dress and sew dresses for people who'd been kind to me. But if I did well and my dresses sold, I could help Papa get you all to Cuba even faster!

Papa looked back at me with a warm smile, nodded to Señora Graciela, and told her I would be happy to take the sewing machine. She clapped her hands and said she'd have it sent over in the afternoon.

As we were about to say goodbye, Doctor Pablo turned to Papa. Pointing to the newspaper on the dining table, he said, "Bad news these days in Europe. Have you heard, Señor Abraham? The Nazis have taken over Austria. They're treating the Hebrews badly. They forced Hebrew actresses in Vienna to scrub toilets while they stood there laughing."

Doctor Pablo called Jewish people "hebreos" rather than "judíos" because he thought that word was more polite.

"You are safe here," Doctor Pablo added, smiling at us.

But Papa and I looked at each other in fear.

"We are safe, but not our family," Papa said.

"You will be together one day," Doctor Pablo said.

"Juntos" was the Spanish word he used for "together." I repeated it to myself to make it come true.

Late in the afternoon, there was a knock on the door, and we found Mario José standing there with a Singer sewing machine. Manuela was with him too.

"Señora Graciela asked me to bring over la Singer," Mario José said. "I help her with her chores when I'm not busy at the sugarcane fields."

We invited them in and I asked Mario José to put the sewing machine in my bedroom so I could sew whenever I wanted without disturbing Papa.

Once it was set up, Papa asked them to sit in the rocking chairs in the living room, and I brought over the bench from the kitchen for Papa and me. Then I went to the room and got some remnants of cloth I still had left to show to Manuela. I asked her which she liked, and she said she liked them all. "Todos, me gustan todos." We both laughed. I unfolded them and we draped them against our bodies to see how they looked. We were wearing the floral dresses I'd made and we were like mirrors for each other.

Mario José asked about our familia and if I had a mamá.

Papa explained about our family in Poland and how they were waiting for us to bring them to Cuba.

Mario José nodded. "Separados por el mar," he said.

Yes, sadly we were separated by the sea from the people we loved most.

Papa should then have asked Mario José about his family, but Papa was not one to ask questions. I was about to when Mario José himself pointed to Manuela and said, "No tiene mamá."

Manuela's face became sad and Mario José told us how his wonderful wife, Cecilia, Manuela's mother, had died two years ago from a heart attack that struck like lightning and took her away so fast there was no time to say goodbye. Ma Felipa had needed to step in and be not only Manuela's grandmother but her mother as well.

I felt sorry for Manuela and reached over to give her a hug.

I thought about Mama and Bubbe, how lucky we are to have them both. I wish I could give them a big hug right now. You all feel so far away.

By then, the afternoon light had faded. Mario José stood and said he and Manuela needed to get home. Ma Felipa was probably wondering why they were gone for so long. They wished us a good night and we did the same, one father and daughter to another father and daughter.

After Papa went to sleep, I sat down to try the sewing machine.

At first it was a disaster. I sewed a seam and it came out

crooked. I had to rip it out and sew it again several times. But once I got the hang of how to step on the treadle, I realized why the sewing machine was such a great invention. I could finish a seam in seconds.

It was harder to sew the buttonholes and attach the sleeves and collars. I kept practicing those tasks as the night stretched before me and the light of the kerosene lamp wore down.

Fortunately, the bobbin had a new spool of thread. I could sew and sew to my heart's content.

By the time the soft light of dawn shone through the window, I'd mastered the basics of the sewing machine and decided it was as dear to me as a fiddle is to a fiddler.

Your loving sister,
ESTHER

AGRAMONTE

March 17, 1938

Dearest Malka,

It's Purim today—and my birthday. I can't believe I'm officially only twelve years old! I feel like I have grown so much since that day three months ago when I vowed to make the journey across the ocean to help Papa.

For the past few days, I've been staying up late sewing and waking up early to sew—I guess I've been practically sewing in my sleep. I think that's how I was able to do so much. Using up a remnant of several yards that I had left, I made dresses in three different sizes—for a little child, a young girl, and an adult woman. They all had buttons down the front and pockets at the hips, with just some variation in the collars, belts, and sashes. My neck and shoulders hurt, but thinking of Mama being proud of my dresses, I could tolerate all the aches and pains.

After Papa was done with his morning prayers, I showed him what I'd been working on. I spread the three sample dresses out on the bed—I thought they looked beautiful.

"You have a great talent, my daughter, just as they say," he told me. "Now let me wish you a happy birthday!" Papa gave me a hug and my favorite flower from the garden—a pink hibiscus, which Cubans call "mar pacífico." I held it gently and watched its winged petals unfurl in my hands.

Later we caught the direct midmorning train to Havana. We didn't know if the Jewish shops would be open on Purim, but they all were. It was Thursday, a regular workday, and no one could afford to lose business.

"What do you want to sell next?" Zvi Mandelbaum said after he paid us our commission. "More sandals? Leather belts? I have a new supply of Christian idols." He laughed and said we were turning out to be his most successful peddlers.

I tugged at Papa's sleeve to remind him of my plan, which I hoped would make us a lot more money than we were earning as peddlers. Poor Papa, who is too kind, stood there sweating, thinking of what to say. Fortunately, a customer came in and Zvi Mandelbaum turned his attention away from us.

"Come, Papa," I whispered, and we ducked out of the store. "Let's go to Rifka Rubenstein's store. I want to show her the dresses."

We wove through the crowds that formed on Calle Muralla in the middle of the day, people strolling not just on the sidewalks but in the middle of the street, their voices sounding musical, rising into the air like joyful melodies.

When we entered the store, Rifka Rubenstein was sitting behind the counter as before, this time reading a Yiddish newspaper. She looked up and greeted us in her chatty way.

"Here you are again, the sweet girl who reminds me of my

granddaughter in Poland." Then she sighed. "Have you seen the news? Look at this! It says the crowds cheered the Nazis as they arrived in Vienna."

She passed the newspaper to us. It was chilling to see the news confirmed in Yiddish, the same news Doctor Pablo had told us about.

"What is going to become of the world?" Rifka Rubenstein exclaimed as she brought her hands to either side of her head and rocked back and forth, a gesture that reminded me of Bubbe.

Papa told her, "We must not lose faith. There is much good in the world too. But we're worried about our loved ones in Poland. We're a long way from having enough savings to bring six members of our family here."

Rifka Rubenstein nodded. "I know how it is. You take food from your own mouth and save and save and it barely adds up to pennies. My husband worked as a peddler for years when we arrived in Cuba, and with much sacrifice, we finally bought this store. We thought our future looked so bright, and then one day he was on top of a ladder getting a bolt of fabric down from a high shelf and fell to the ground, breaking his skull. It was the saddest day of my life. I have my son and his wife and three grandchildren in Poland, but they don't want to come to Cuba. They say if I go to New York, then they'll come and live with me. So I've applied for a visa to the United States. Who knows if it will ever arrive? If it does, I will go immediately, and then I will send for my family, and finally we will be together." She paused before she asked, "But tell me, what can I do for you? Have you come for more fabric?"

I reached into my satchel and pulled out the three dresses. I held one up at a time, starting with the smallest and moving to the biggest.

Rifka Rubenstein watched in wonder. "You made these yourself? My, oh my, you have blessed hands."

"Our neighbor gave me a sewing machine and I have been experimenting," I said.

She examined the seams and collars and buttons and belts and sashes. "Such original designs you've come up with. And pockets too!"

"These are samples," I told her. "I want to buy more fabric and make dresses to sell in the countryside. I think they'll sell if I keep the prices low."

"These dresses are elegant. You don't need to sell them in the countryside, my dear," Rifka Rubenstein replied. "I am sure they'd sell here in Havana. Why don't I give you some fabric and you can make dresses I can sell in my store? I'll hang these three dresses up in the window, and I'm sure customers will come."

That was such an exciting idea, I leaped with joy. With Papa's help, we hung the dresses in the shop window and Rifka Rubenstein added a for-sale sign: A LA VENTA.

Within half an hour, passersby were stopping and peering at the dresses. I thought I was dreaming! Then they started to come in and ask for prices. We had not even discussed that.

I had thought to sell them for fifty cents in Agramonte. But Rifka Rubenstein thought they were worth more. She said they cost two pesos for the children's sizes and five pesos for the women's. I guess those prices were a bargain in Havana! Rifka Rubenstein took orders for ten dresses and promised they would be ready by the following week.

I was going to have a lot of work, but I was thrilled. The more dresses I make, the faster we'll get you to Cuba!

When it was time for lunch, Rifka Rubenstein closed up the store and invited us to eat with her. "You won't have to go far. I live in the apartment right above the store."

Papa and I agreed and followed her to the apartment. It had colorful Spanish-tiled floors, a living room, three small bedrooms, a small kitchen with a refrigerator, and an indoor toilet with running water. What I liked the best was the balcony. I stood there with Papa, looking out over the narrow streets of Havana. On the horizon, the sea glittered like a row of sequins. The enormous sea that separates us.

Soon we smelled delicious aromas from the kitchen. Rifka Rubenstein invited us to her table and served us chicken soup with kreplach, brisket with potatoes, and even a raisin kugel. We ate like beggars, not so much because we were ravenous, though we were, but because we hadn't eaten food like this for so long, food that tasted like Bubbe's cooking—which reminded us of home.

Afterward we sat by the balcony, feeling the breeze from

the sea. Papa said, "Thank you, Rifka. We have enjoyed your lunch and are grateful for your generosity. But I don't know if my daughter can make all the dresses you have promised. She is only a girl of twelve."

Why was Papa saying such things? Of course I could make all the dresses that Rifka Rubenstein promised. And many more too! I tried not to feel angry. Papa cared about me and wanted to make clear I was still a young person and shouldn't be taking on the burdens of an adult. But in times of emergency, a child must rise up and act older than her years, don't you think?

"Papa, I can do it! Please don't worry, Mrs. Rubenstein. I can sew quickly—and I like doing it. But it's true that I am only one person. Papa, do you think you could cut the fabric? I have the patterns already made. If we work together, I can finish all the orders in a week. Then we can take more orders."

"Of course I will cut the fabric, Esther," Papa said. "That's a wonderful plan. We can be a team."

Rifka Rubenstein smiled at us. "I will gladly take all the dresses you can make. And on this first order from today, to show my goodwill, I will not take a commission. All the earnings will be for the two of you. And afterward, I promise I will only ask for a small amount so that you can save and bring your family to Cuba."

"Thank you, thank you!" I said in Yiddish. Because we were in Cuba, I then said, "Muchas gracias."

Papa stood. "Now we must be going. We have a train to catch."

Rifka Rubenstein smiled. "It's time to open the store again. Come, let's choose some fabric before you go."

She gave me lots of light cotton fabric, plus some miracle cloth that doesn't wrinkle, and we squeezed it into our satchels. And she gave me more buttons and needles and thread and a bit of lace.

Then Papa and I ran off to catch the last train back to Agramonte. Papa slept the whole way, but I wanted to guard over the fabric and supplies. I stayed awake, squeezing my satchel to my heart. It contained the most precious gem of all—hope and hope and hope.

With all my love,
ESTHER

AGRAMONTE

March 21, 1938

Dearest Malka,

Papa and I have been working constantly. We barely go out, except to buy bread and eggs and milk on Calle Independencia. We have ten dresses to make that will earn us much more money than we get from peddling. If we keep going, we'll have all of you here very soon! But Papa insisted we rest on Saturday and respect our Shabbos. He prayed and sat in the yard, contemplating the trees and the flowers. I daydreamed about dresses, how I'd change collars or pockets to create different looks.

Our neighbors must have been wondering what we were doing indoors. They had gotten used to seeing us with our satchels, roaming about the town and trudging on the dirt roads leading to the sugar mill. Late on Sunday afternoon, Señora Graciela knocked on our door to ask if we were well. She was wearing the black dress I'd made for her and I could see her white handkerchiefs sticking out of the pockets. I meant to tell her how much I appreciated her gift of the sewing machine, but I was so busy making the dresses, I had not had a chance to knock on her door.

She was stunned to see how the house had been turned upside down with our sewing. Dresses in different stages of completion were scattered on the kitchen table and on the floor of the living room.

"This has become a factory!" she said. "Una fábrica."

From the way she said the word "fábrica," I wondered if we were doing something wrong.

I said, "No, no fábrica. Papa and me."

I was happy when she smiled and said she was glad we were well. And then she invited us to come to dinner the next day.

Papa and I stood at the door as she turned in the direction of her house. In that same moment, Señor Eduardo appeared on his whinnying horse. He stared at us so coldly it gave me the shivers. He didn't say it, but I knew the word "judíos" was on the tip of his tongue. He got off the horse and accompanied Señora Graciela to her house.

We shut the door and kept on sewing, rushing to finish the dresses we had promised by the end of the week.

I tried not to think about Señor Eduardo, but he scared me. All I had to do was recall his icy glare to get chills, though it was as hot and humid as ever.

With all my love as always,

ESTHER

AGRAMONTE

March 24, 1938

Dear Malka,

Last night I stayed up late while Papa slept, adding the finishing touches to the dresses. After making sure they were perfect, I used the remnant of paisley fabric Rifka Rubenstein had given me to sew one more dress so I'd have a new sample to show. I added a wide sash that could be tied in a bow in the front or the back. I folded the dresses carefully, separating them into the different sizes and styles. I added layers of tracing paper to keep them neat. When Papa was done with his prayers, we divided the dresses and packed them into our satchels.

We took the train to Havana and went directly to Rifka Rubenstein's store. The first three sample dresses I made were still hanging in the shop window. Papa and I waited while she helped a customer. When Rifka Rubenstein was done, she put up a sign that said CERRADO so customers would know the store was closed.

"Come with me," she said, and led us to the office in the back.

"We have more orders! Women have been stopping in all

week asking about the dresses. I have never seen anything like it!" Rifka Rubenstein exclaimed.

Papa said, "That is wonderful news, but Esther has worked very hard, day and night. I have done what I could to help by cutting the fabric and keeping things organized, but that is nothing compared to Esther's labor. I don't know how she managed to make so many dresses in one week!" He turned to me with a worried look. "Can you really keep going at this rate?"

"Of course I can, Papa! I even made an additional dress last night while you slept, just to try a few new things."

I carefully took out the dress and held it up in the air so Rifka Rubenstein could see the details. Her eyes glistened as she marveled at my handiwork.

"You have outdone yourself! I am sure all of these dresses will be adored by the people who wear them," she said.

She reached into a safe box, which was hidden behind a chair, and pulled out a wad of bills. She counted out eighty pesos.

"Here's a little extra money for all your efforts."

I passed the money to Papa for safekeeping. Then Rifka Rubenstein said, "So I've taken orders for another twenty-five dresses. Everyone loves the design, because the dresses can be easily adjusted to anyone's measurements. It is a lot of sewing, even for a magician like you, Esther. That is why I told the customers the orders would take a little longer, two weeks or so rather than one."

Papa kissed my forehead and said a prayer for my good health. "Oh, my dear child, you have come to Cuba to exhaust your eyesight and strain your neck and hands. But what can we do? If you are willing, it is the only way we'll ever save our family. If they only knew the sacrifices you are making to bring them here!"

"Papa, I do it with my heart, my entire heart," I said, and I meant it.

"I too am grateful God put you in my path," Rifka Rubenstein remarked. "Now, I must tell you I've raised the prices of the dresses. You will earn a little more and I will earn a commission to cover the cost of the fabric and my other expenses. The dresses are still a steal. I don't think you can find a handmade dress with so much charm and so much practicality anywhere else in Havana. This afternoon the women will be coming to pick up their dresses, and I can't wait to see the smiles on their faces!"

I wished I could see the women's smiles too. But that was impossible. Rifka Rubenstein explained that it would be better if the women didn't know a Jewish refugee girl from Poland was making their dresses. "We'll pretend it's a designer from New York. Is that all right with you?" she said.

I wanted to say no, it wasn't all right. The dresses were my creation, the work of my hands. But we needed the money and we needed it quickly, so I agreed.

Rifka Rubenstein gave us more fabric and buttons, an even

better selection than the last time. We couldn't fit it all into our two satchels, so she gave us each a suitcase. Our bags were very heavy, and we must have looked like two mules walking through Havana! Papa was disappointed we couldn't stop to pray at the synagogue or buy a loaf of challah, as we were so weighed down.

We squeezed onto the crowded train with our belongings. As usual, Papa slept, snoring blissfully, but I couldn't even close my eyes. This time I had brought José Martí's *Simple Verses* to read and perfect my Spanish. I stared at the words, whispering them slowly to myself. I didn't understand the poems very well, but there were many words I now knew—"tierra," land; "flores," flowers; "vida," life; "hojas," leaves; "cielo," sky; "corazón," heart—and I felt proud of all that I'd learned without going to school. I hoped one day I would no longer be a refugee and Spanish would slip from my tongue as easily as a cubana.

Finally we arrived in Agramonte. We lugged the bags to our house. We had barely finished washing our hands when we were startled by a loud knock at the door. I heard a horse neighing and had a bad feeling.

Papa opened the door and there was Señor Eduardo—with a policeman! They rudely pushed Papa aside and entered our home. Señor Eduardo pointed to the satchels and ordered Papa to open them.

Papa did as he was asked. Señor Eduardo reached in and

pulled out fabric and buttons and lace, throwing everything on the floor.

After he finished making a mess, he turned to me and said, "¿Dónde está la máquina de coser?"

I took him to my bedroom and showed him the sewing machine, standing in front of it, trying to protect it with my body. If he took it away, what would we do? But instead, Señor Eduardo turned to Papa and said, "Dame el dinero."

He was demanding Papa give him his money! Papa looked dumbfounded. Why did Papa have to give him any money?

Then came the accusation: I was a refugee and a child and I was working illegally in Cuba. Señor Eduardo said if he reported us, the government would take everything—the fabric, the sewing machine—and charge us a hefty fine. They would put Papa in jail for letting me work. Afterward they would send us back to Poland, where we belonged. They didn't need any more Jews in Cuba. The Jews that Cuba had taken in out of pity were too many.

"Fuera, judíos," he said in conclusion—and I understood what Señor Eduardo really wanted. He wanted to hurt us. He had wanted to hurt us from the moment he saw us walking along the country paths leading to his sugar mill. He had wanted to hurt us simply because we were Jewish. He had been waiting for the right moment and the right excuse. And he found it.

The policeman yanked Papa's arms and twisted them behind his back. Señor Eduardo reached into Papa's pocket and pulled out the eighty pesos we had received today from Rifka Rubenstein, all the money we had earned from the dresses I had sewn, all the money that was going toward bringing you and Mama and Bubbe and my brothers to Cuba.

Señor Eduardo counted out the bills, gave some to the policeman, and took the rest for himself. Then he threw ten pesos on the floor and stepped on them.

"Recógelo, judío," he said to Papa, and tried to force him to get down on his knees and pick up the money from under his boot.

Poor Papa was trembling like a leaf. I wouldn't let Señor Eduardo humiliate my sweet papa like that.

"No!" I yelled, and bent down myself and got the money as the two men walked out laughing.

Papa felt broken by everything that had happened. I told him to pray, that prayers always helped, but he said he couldn't, not today. I told him things would be better tomorrow. He went to bed and fell asleep right away.

I am awake, unable to sleep, writing to you, dear Malka, on this sad night. From a distance, I hear a lone dog barking, lost and hungry. I try to remember that most Cubans are not like Señor Eduardo. I have met so many people with big hearts on this island, where every day feels like summer, and their kindness is like sunshine. I console myself as much as I can with that thought.

Now I will say good night and close my eyes and dream of a new day.

With my love as always,
ESTHER

AGRAMONTE

March 25, 1938

Dear Malka,

I fell asleep just before dawn. When I woke up, I went searching for Papa. It was reassuring to find him praying. I was afraid he had lost faith in his prayers. For Papa, that would be the end of everything.

His shoulders ached from the brutal way he had been pushed and yanked around. I asked Papa to let me go ask Doctor Pablo if he had an ointment to soothe the pain. He agreed but told me not to be gone too long or he would worry.

Doctor Pablo saw patients at the pharmacy next door to his house. It was still early in the morning and no one was there yet.

"¿Qué pasa, Esther?" he asked.

"Dolores," I said, and pointed to my shoulders. Then I added, "Papa."

He excused himself and went to a back room. After a few moments, he returned with a small jar of an ointment he had mixed up himself and told me Papa should rub it on his shoulders. I had brought the ten pesos I had picked up off the floor, but Doctor Pablo wouldn't accept any money. He said he would come and see Papa when he closed the pharmacy.

I swung past the grocery store. I called out buenos días to Juan Chang, who was sitting behind the counter, and he said buenos días back to me.

I kept walking, eager to get back to Papa and give him the ointment. Just before I reached the corner, I heard someone calling me by my name.

"Esther!"

I turned and there was Francisco Chang. "Ven, por favor."

He motioned for me, politely, to please go back with him to the store. I wondered what for and hesitated. But Francisco repeated "por favor" with such gentleness, I turned around and followed him.

Inside the store, Juan Chang asked if Papa and I were doing well and getting accustomed to life in Cuba. After the horrible ordeal we'd been through with Señor Eduardo, it was hard for me to lie and say everything was fine. I stuttered as I said, "Bien, gracias," knowing I didn't sound very convincing.

Juan Chang reached under the counter and passed me a little square tin.

I was surprised to see it was sour cherry tea. The kind that came from Poland. Bubbe loved this tea, but it was a luxury, so we only got it now and then. Do you remember this tea, Malka? It was so tart it made your mouth pucker. Now Juan Chang was insisting I take this tea as a gift, this tea that had come all the way from Poland, just as I had.

"Té polaco," he said, and smiled.

Polish tea.

Last night Papa and I suffered terribly, and this morning Juan Chang was offering me Polish sour cherry tea. Yes, the world was full of surprises.

I felt unsure about accepting this gift, but how could I refuse Juan Chang's kindness? He wanted to show me he understood what it was like to be far from everything that was familiar.

"Gracias," I said. "Muchas gracias."

Juan Chang nodded in his kindly way and asked Francisco to wrap the tin in brown paper. Francisco took his time. When he was done, he passed the parcel to me. And he passed me something else: a rolled-up piece of paper. I opened it and saw a beautiful drawing of a palm tree. Every detail of the trunk and the leaves was clear and distinct. So Francisco liked to draw! I smiled and said, "Bonito," and he smiled back.

"Adiós," I said, wishing I could explain what had happened with Señor Eduardo and why I had to rush. Another day I would ask if Francisco had more sketches. Now I needed to give Papa a balm for his wounds and a taste of home.

Papa was still in pain, but he said praying had helped calm his soul. I gave him the ointment and told him to rest and spread it on his shoulders. "I am not ill!" he said, but he did as I asked and soon fell asleep.

I boiled water so I could brew tea for Papa when he woke up. Then I toasted the bread so it would be crispy and good for dunking in the tea.

I picked up the scissors and started cutting fabric to make

the dresses that had been ordered. I had twenty-five dresses to finish in two weeks, and the sooner I got going, the better.

But I thought of how much I wanted to make another dress for Manuela and myself, so I decided to start with that. There was an apron hanging from a hook in the kitchen, and I took it down, slipped it over my head, and knotted the bow at my waist to see how it was put together. It occurred to me I could make a wraparound-style dress, like the apron, that could tie at the waist with a thin sash and fit people of many different shapes and sizes—and I'd save time by not sewing on buttons or making buttonholes. I had light blue fabric and got started on Manuela's dress. Then for my own dress I'd use sunflower-yellow fabric, brighter than anything I've ever worn.

I was concentrating so intensely making these dresses that I didn't notice Papa had woken up until he stood by my side.

"Papa, come have some tea and toast," I said.

"Where did you get tea?"

"Sit down and I'll tell you."

Papa sat down and savored the tart flavor that had traveled to Cuba from so far away. "Sour cherry tea. I haven't had this in years."

I told him about Juan Chang and Francisco Chang, how the uncle had given me the tin and the nephew had given me the drawing of the palm tree—one giving me something of Poland and the other something of Cuba.

"They are very kind and I am grateful they have shown concern for you," Papa said. "But you must not get too close, dear Esther. Remember you are Jewish and we're only here in Agramonte for a brief while. You mustn't set down roots or it will hurt when we have to leave. Be cordial to everyone who is cordial to you. And know that one day we will be in Havana with other Jews again, not here in the wilderness by ourselves."

It hurt to hear Papa say this, but I understood. I nodded and said, "Yes, Papa, I know."

"I brought you here and I must make sure you don't get swept away and forget you are a Jewish girl."

A knock on the door interrupted us. We were relieved to find it was Doctor Pablo, and I was glad I had something to offer a guest. I gave him a cup of the sour cherry tea and made sure to tell him to add sugar, because I had learned that Cubans liked everything sweet. He took a few sips and said it was very good, and then they went to the bedroom so Doctor Pablo could examine Papa. When they came back out, they sat in the rocking chairs in the living room like old friends.

"La verdad," Doctor Pablo said. He wanted to know the truth. How had he gotten those ugly bruises?

Papa kept silent.

"Señor Eduardo," I said.

Just saying the name aloud made me afraid.

Papa wouldn't talk, so I told the story as best I could, trying to remember all the terrifying words Señor Eduardo had used. I told him how Señor Eduardo had again said to us, "Fuera, judíos." Doctor Pablo listened intently. And when I got to the part about Señor Eduardo reaching into Papa's pocket and snatching his money, Doctor Pablo became furious.

He rose so quickly from the rocking chair he knocked it over. He said he wouldn't permit Señor Eduardo to keep mistreating us or for Nazis to take over Cuba!

As he took his leave, Doctor Pablo shook Papa's hand and told him to keep using the ointment and he'd be better in a few days. Then he turned to me and said to keep on sewing, and those words comforted me.

I will keep sewing, day and night, and in my sleep too. I won't let anyone stop me, dear Malka! I will make a bridge of dresses so that you can cross the ocean, and you know I will be waiting here on the other side.

With my sincere and
everlasting love,
Esther

AGRAMONTE

March 28, 1938

Dear Malka,

I don't want to brag, dear little sister, but those two wrap-around dresses I started making the other day turned out very well! I've stumbled upon a style that's simple to sew and easy to wear. It only took a moment for me to wrap the sunflower-yellow dress around myself and tie a bow on the side to secure it.

This afternoon, while Papa took his nap, I dashed out to give Manuela her new dress. As I approached Ma Felipa's house, I heard the sound of drums. The voices of women singing rose into the air. I made out the familiar words: "Yemayá Asesu, Asesu Yemayá . . ."

Women, men, and children were crowded at the door, swaying to the music. I didn't want to barge in, so I just stood there with them. Before long, Manuela spotted me and pulled me inside.

There were three men playing drums of different sizes that rested sideways on their laps—I learned they were called batá drums—and Mario José played the largest one. Manuela explained that these drums were very old, and through them they called to the ancestors who had survived the sufferings of slavery to thank them and to say they'd never forget them.

Ma Felipa led the singing and the women repeated her words in a chorus. She was wearing the dress I had made for her and lots of colorful beaded necklaces. After a while, she began to dance in a small circle next to her Yemayá fountain.

Manuela squeezed my hand.

"Baila," she said.

Dance.

I tried to imitate Manuela's steps, feeling awkward at first. But then I listened to the drums and the singing and let myself move back and forth to the music.

Suddenly Ma Felipa stopped dancing, the drumming stopped, and everyone froze. Her body was shaking and she had closed her eyes. She bowed toward the batá drums and then greeted everyone in an African language. Several women came to her side and walked her around the room. She left for a moment and returned with a bright blue shawl around her shoulders. Everyone greeted her as if they were meeting her for the first time.

Then she began to dance and the drums started up again. As she twisted and turned, her shawl moved like sea waves around her.

Yemayá, they called her. Not Ma Felipa. She had become Yemayá.

Finally, she grew tired from the dancing and a woman offered her water from the fountain in a gourd. Then the crowd drifted outside and formed a circle around the ceiba tree. They had white flowers in their hands, and one by one they placed them within the loops of the chain that encircled the ceiba tree.

I suddenly realized I'd left Papa napping and hadn't told him where I was going. If he woke up, he'd be worried about me.

"Manuela," I said.

She turned and smiled. I was still holding the dress I'd made for her. I'd rolled it up and tied it together with a ribbon of fabric. I didn't want to give it to Manuela in front of all the people.

She understood and led me out to the street, where I gave her my gift. She untied the ribbon and the dress spilled out.

"Bonito, bonito," she said.

She was wearing the floral dress I'd made for her, and she put the new dress over it. She smiled when she saw how it wrapped around her waist and held together with just the tie. Then we said goodbye and I rushed to get back to Papa.

I found Papa, scissors in hand, cutting fabric.

"Papa, I'm so glad you're feeling strong enough to work again."

"Where have you been, my child?" he asked.

"I went to give Manuela the new dress I made for her. There were a lot of people at her house. They had drums and everyone was dancing and singing."

"That's part of their religion. They brought it from Africa. And they let you stay?"

"Yes, Papa, they all knew who I was and didn't mind my being there. I even danced a little."

"Esther, as I've told you, don't forget you're a Jew."

"I always remember, Papa."

I didn't say it aloud, not to contradict Papa, but I was grateful I had heard the drums. I could never forget I am a Jew. But the sound of the drums at Ma Felipa's house was now in my life and I was sure it would never leave me.

One day you too will hear the drums when you come to Cuba, and they will change you, my dear sister.

Your older sister,
who loves you,
Esther

AGRAMONTE

April 12, 1938

Dear Malka,

We were a few days late bringing the dresses to Rifka Rubenstein, but she didn't make a fuss, as the dresses had all come out beautifully.

This time, when Rifka Rubenstein paid us, we asked if we could keep most of our money in her safe box. When we told her we had been robbed, Rifka Rubenstein was horrified. "I'm so sorry. I will give you a little extra to help make up for what you lost. Of course you can keep your money here. My safe box is always locked and no one has the key except me."

"Thank you," Papa said. "That will take a weight off our shoulders."

She smiled and said, "I have taken orders for forty dresses. Can you believe it? Some of the women have come back for a second or a third dress. They say the dresses fit so well and are so comfortable and so stylish, coming from New York. Little do they know the dresses are made right here in Cuba! They even say the dresses rival those of El Encanto—the most expensive department store in Havana! Isn't that wonderful?"

She paused and asked, "Could you finish this order by the end of next month? That will give you more time."

I looked at Papa to see if he agreed. When he nodded, so did I.

"Very good," Rifka Rubenstein said. "I know you will want to take a few days off for Passover. I am going to my cousin's for both seders or I would invite you here."

When she mentioned Passover, I got homesick for our seders in Govorovo, when we were all together. Remember how emotional Papa would get when he spoke of our ancestors being slaves in Egypt? He would talk about the suffering of all those who came before us as if he'd been there and gone through it himself.

I put these thoughts aside as Rifka Rubenstein gave us the fabric and buttons and lace and thread that we needed to complete the next order of dresses. I was happy my dresses were selling so well, but it hurt that no one could know the dresses were my creation. I decided, right then and there, that I would put a label in all the new dresses that would say "Designs by Esther."

After we left, Papa and I stopped at the synagogue for matzo. An old man with a long white beard and a dark black coat sat at a desk in the office, with boxes of matzo piled up against the wall behind him. He gave Papa a friendly greeting when we came in, then told him, "Well, Avrum, I can only give you two boxes today. The donation from the American Jews is not so large this year."

"That's all right," Papa told him. "It's only two of us for now, until we've saved up enough to bring my wife and my mother and my other four children here. This is my daughter Esther, and we are working so hard you cannot imagine." Papa smiled at me and continued, "So we will manage fine with two boxes of matzo. And hope that next year the rest of my family is here and that the American Jews will be more generous with their brothers and sisters who haven't had the good fortune to land with them in the Golden Medina."

Papa stuffed the two boxes of matzo into his satchel, and then I asked him if we could make a stop at El Encanto.

"Please, Papa, I'm so curious to have a look! It will just be for a minute."

"It is a store for rich people, but how can I say no to you, my dear child? Of course we will go, even though it is in the opposite direction of the train station."

I have never seen anything like El Encanto, Malka! The store was as magnificent as a palace, and guards stood at the main entrance to open the doors for the sophisticated shoppers who streamed in and out. Those who happened to glance at Papa and me weighed down with all our shmattes quickly turned their heads in embarrassment. I felt small and unimportant, like a fly to be swatted away.

Papa was patient and walked around the outside of the store with me so I could stare at the shop windows. The women mannequins had on slinky evening gowns, and the young girl ones wore frilly dresses that looked stiff and uncomfortable.

There were no dresses like mine that were both elegant and practical in any of the windows.

I was so lost in thought, I didn't notice how long my nose was pressed to one of the windows. A guard came over and tapped me on the shoulder and motioned for Papa and me to get moving.

We were worn to the bone when we arrived back at the train station and collapsed into our seats. After being on our feet all afternoon, the hard wooden benches on the second-class train actually felt cozy. While Papa slept, I stayed awake and watchful as always. I tried to read José Martí's poems to keep improving my Spanish, but I couldn't concentrate. All around me were other worried-looking people, keeping a watchful eye on their own bundles.

I thought about the carefree shoppers I saw streaming in and out of El Encanto. Why is the world divided into rich and poor? Why can't there be enough for everyone? Why does a whole sea have to separate me from you, dear Malka?

With my sincere
love as always,
Esther

AGRAMONTE

April 15, 1938

Dear Malka,

Maybe it was a foolish idea, but I asked Papa if I could invite some guests to our Passover seder tonight.

"Who will you invite, Esther? There isn't another Jew for miles and miles."

"Do they have to be Jewish to come to our seder?"

"But we're not even going to have a true seder. We don't have wine or a shank bone for the seder plate."

"We have eggs. And I can find bitter herbs in the yard. We have an onion that I will cut up so everyone can dip it in salt water."

"And tell me, Esther, what will we offer them to eat after the seder? We barely have enough for ourselves."

"There are pineapples and coconuts and bananas growing everywhere. There is plenty of guava paste. And of course there is sugarcane."

"That is not a proper Passover meal."

"Papa, we're in Cuba and we need to do things the Cuban way."

"And who do you want to invite?"

"I want to invite Doctor Pablo and Señora Graciela, Ma Felipa, Mario José, and Manuela, and Juan Chang and his nephew Francisco Chang."

Papa looked at me as if I were crazy.

"Esther, haven't you noticed black people and white people in this town don't like to be together? And Chinese people keep to themselves, like us."

"They may be different from one another, but they are the ones who've been kind to me in Agramonte. That's why I want to invite them all. Papa, please . . ."

His shook his head, but he agreed, and I rushed out to invite them. It was hard to explain what a seder was. I called it a "fiesta hebrea." But that only made sense to Doctor Pablo, so I said it was a "fiesta de los polacos." A Polish party! And everyone agreed to come.

We had just enough mismatched plates for the nine of us. And miraculously we had exactly ten cups, so I could even put one out for Elijah. I'd have to explain to my guests that the tradition is to pour an extra cup of wine and leave the door open in case he shows up as an unexpected guest. But what would we drink? I remembered we had the sour cherry tea. I would brew a big pot, let it cool, and add lots of sugar so it would almost taste like wine.

When I realized we had no tablecloth, I made one by sewing some cloth remnants together, and I also made napkins.

Then I gathered up our fabric and supplies and put them in my bedroom, leaving no trace of the lint and scraps and the mess that had become ordinary since I'd begun making dresses.

Shortly before dusk, Doctor Pablo and Señora Graciela arrived. Señora Graciela wore the black dress I made for her. She greeted me with a sad smile and I wondered if she was thinking of her daughter, Emilia. While Papa and Doctor Pablo chatted in the living room, she took my hand and we stepped aside. She peered into my bedroom and saw the fabric and the supplies I had stashed in a corner of the room. Then she ran her hand over the sewing machine.

"You are happy with the sewing machine?" she asked.

I told her I loved it and would always be grateful to her for her gift.

Tears filled her eyes and she said, "Lo siento."

Why was she saying she was sorry?

I didn't understand every word she said, but she mentioned Señor Eduardo, and I understood that she knew what had happened and felt bad. Without expecting he would be vicious, she had told Señor Eduardo about the sewing machine and how talented I was at dressmaking.

"Lo siento, mi niña," she repeated, and hugged me.

We stepped back into the living room and heard a soft knock on the door. It was Juan and Francisco Chang. They looked embarrassed as they politely nodded and said, "Buenas noches." Doctor Pablo and Señora Graciela also looked embarrassed. Then another soft knock sounded and there were Ma Felipa, Mario José, and Manuela, looking embarrassed too. What had I done by bringing such different people together? Was Papa right to warn me?

I led everyone to the table. I had placed a chair at the head for Papa, and the rest of us would have to squeeze onto the benches on either side. I asked Doctor Pablo and Señora Graciela to sit on the same bench as Ma Felipa and Mario José, and I sat with Juan Chang, Francisco, and Manuela on the other.

I lit the Shabbos candles and then Papa began the seder. "Tonight we remember the suffering of the Hebrews when we were slaves in Egypt," he said.

Ma Felipa looked astonished. "Who were the Hebrews? You mean the polacos, like yourselves?"

Papa nodded. "Yes, our ancestors were slaves in Egypt."

"I never knew the Hebrews were slaves. I was also enslaved when I was a young woman."

Mario José gently patted Ma Felipa's hand. "Mamá, you can tell your story another time. We are going to hear the story of the Hebrews tonight."

Señora Graciela, who was sitting next to Ma Felipa, started to fidget. Her elbow bumped into Ma Felipa as she reached for a handkerchief in her pocket to wipe the sweat from her brow. "Lo siento," she told Ma Felipa.

"Are you sorry for bumping into me or for coming from a

family that owned slaves on your sugar mill?" Ma Felipa said. "A family that once owned me?"

I understood every painful word Ma Felipa had spoken.

Señora Graciela replied, "Lo siento todo."

She was sorry for everything.

Juan Chang looked across the table, and in a whisper, he said, "There were Chinese slaves too at the sugar mill."

Francisco also spoke quietly as he said to his uncle, "That was a long time ago."

Manuela said, "My grandmother was enslaved and I was born free."

There was an awkward silence.

Mario José turned to Papa. "We should let Señor Abraham continue now."

Papa held up his cup and the others did the same with theirs. Papa said the prayer and drank the sour cherry tea. We all followed him.

I brought a bowl and a pitcher filled with water for us to wash our hands. Then Papa said another prayer.

Papa instructed everyone to dip a piece of onion into the cup of salt water. As we did so, he explained, "Agua salada para las lágrimas de los esclavos."

Salt water for the tears of the enslaved.

I remembered the ceiba tree in Ma Felipa's yard, the tree that cries.

Papa held up the matzo and explained that when the Hebrews escaped from Egypt, they didn't have time to wait for the bread to rise, and so they ate unleavened bread.

He gave everyone a piece of matzo and told us to eat it first with the bitter herbs, then with a slice of the thick candied guava paste.

Papa said, "We eat something bitter first to remember the sadness of the Hebrews and then something sweet to remember the happiness of the Hebrews, because we were slaves and then we were free."

Ma Felipa asked for an extra slice of guava paste. "I am glad we are all free people. May slavery never exist again."

"Amen," Papa said.

"Amen," repeated Ma Felipa, Juan Chang, and all the rest of us.

Then I brought the fruit that Papa and I had prepared to the table, along with the eggs and the sugarcane, and served everybody.

As we ate, I thought about what to say to my guests. I remembered how everyone in Cuba loved the poems of José Martí. Slowly, pronouncing each word carefully, I recited the verse about the leopard who is happy in his den in the forest, staying warm and dry. But then Martí says,

Yo tengo más que el leopardo
Porque tengo un buen amigo.

I have more than the leopard
Because I have a good friend.

To our guests, who had joined Papa and me for Passover without knowing what a Jewish girl from Poland was asking of them, I said, "You are all my good friends. I want to say gracias."

Doctor Pablo chuckled. "Look at that, la polaquita has already learned to recite the poems of our beloved José Martí!" Everyone laughed. Then he added, "Esther, you don't need to say gracias. I am glad you and your father chose to live in Agramonte."

Ma Felipa chimed in, "We are happy you are with us."

Juan Chang said, "I have more sour cherry tea in from Poland. Don't be shy about asking for another tin."

Manuela and Francisco squeezed a little closer to me.

Then Doctor Pablo told us he had something he wanted to say.

"Tonight, Esther invited us and we all came separately, not knowing we'd sit together at the same table. We came because we've seen what good people she and her father are. They are here in Cuba working hard to bring over their family. They've come as immigrants because the land they're from no longer welcomes them. The situation of the Hebrews is growing worse day by day in Europe. The Nazis have taken over Austria and they will not stop there. You've heard of Hitler—he's spreading hatred of the Jewish people. Now there are people in Cuba who are starting to think like Hitler. In my own family, I have seen this hatred."

Señora Graciela chimed in, "It is my brother, Eduardo. We are so sorry for how horribly he has treated Esther and Señor Abraham."

Ma Felipa responded, "I caught him trying to hurt Señor Abraham on the road by my house. I thought he was being mean in his usual way. I didn't know it was because he hates the Hebrews."

"I am ashamed he's my brother," Señora Graciela said, bowing her head.

Doctor Pablo spoke again. "Maybe it seems impossible, but one day Hitler or his followers might want to take over Cuba. We must not lose our beautiful island to people who want to spread hatred."

Mario José asked, "What can we do?"

"We can't allow Nazis here!" Manuela said. "Or for Señor Eduardo to hurt Esther or Señor Abraham."

Francisco spoke up in his soft, polite way. "What if we form a society? The Anti-Nazi Society of Agramonte."

"That's a good idea! Even if the members are just us," I said.

"There will be more than just us. I'm the leader of the union at the sugar mill and will speak to the workers. We'll call a strike if Señor Eduardo tries anything," Mario José announced.

Señora Graciela shuddered. "But, Mario José, a strike would stop the sugar production and the workers would lose their pay."

Mario José replied, "We've known each other since we were children, Graciela, so I hope you don't mind me speaking frankly. You are different from your brother and I appreciate that. If it's the workers you are concerned about, they've been ready to call a strike for a long time because of the miserable conditions at the sugar mill. They work themselves to the bone cutting the cane and boiling the molasses and can barely feed their families."

"I understand," Señora Graciela said. "If you must strike, I will be on your side, Mario José. I must do what is good, even if it means being against my own flesh and blood."

Doctor Pablo looked around the table. "As of today, then, we're all members of the Anti-Nazi Society of Agramonte. Do you agree?"

We all said yes, and before Doctor Pablo left, he told us, "Our society will be following in the footsteps of the anthropologist Fernando Ortiz. Last year he started an association in Cuba to educate people so they're not afraid of cultures that are different from their own. He says hatred comes from ignorance. That's why it's good to learn about each other's customs and traditions. Thank you, Esther and Señor Abraham, for sharing yours with us tonight."

Then everyone said, "Hasta mañana," and I felt at peace, hoping for a tomorrow filled with kindness.

Afterward, Papa and I sat in the rocking chairs.

"You see, Papa, everything went well."

"Fortunately, yes, Esther. But tomorrow night, let's have a quiet seder, just the two of us."

"Of course, Papa."

I hope you and Mama and Bubbe and my brothers have had a good seder, with plenty of matzo.

Sending all my love,
ESTHER

AGRAMONTE

May 5, 1938

Dear Malka,

The rainy season's begun and I've never seen so much rain come pouring from the sky all at once. An umbrella doesn't help at all—you still end up soaking wet. The storms usually occur in the afternoon and clear very suddenly, losing their fury all at once. The sun reappears and the countryside turns the brightest green.

Rainy days are good for sewing, and the last few weeks have been a frenzy of work to finish the next order of dresses for Rifka Rubenstein. But Papa and I have been in a cheerful mood and each day he insists we take a break. So while Papa prays or naps, I go to Manuela's or visit with Francisco Chang at the store.

I've learned many new jump-rope rhymes with Manuela. One that we like a lot goes like this:

Caballito blanco,
Llévame de aquí.
Llévame a mi casa,
Donde yo nací.

Little white pony,
Take me away from here.
Take me home,
Where I was born.

We play and laugh, and when we get too hot and sweaty, Ma Felipa gives us a delicious coconut sweet. We talk about our dreams too.

"My father is saving to send me away to school next year," Manuela tells me. "I really want to go so that I can become a teacher, but I'll miss my father and grandmother so much. They're the only family I have."

"I'm so sorry your mother died."

"She's not here to hug me anymore, but I feel her inside me, encouraging me."

"Your mother would be proud of you," I told Manuela, and this brought a few tears to her eyes.

I reached into my pocket and gave her a lace-trimmed handkerchief I'd made with a leftover square of linen. It wasn't embroidered like one of Bubbe's handkerchiefs, but it still reminded me of her.

"How pretty!" Manuela said. "Everything you sew is beautiful, even the simplest things. You are already such a good dressmaker, Esther! When you grow up, you will be even more amazing."

"Right now, it's hard to think of who I'll be when I grow up. I just want my family to be safe and make it to Cuba."

"We'll keep fighting against the Nazis here so your family will have a safe home when they arrive."

"Gracias, Manuela. I'll always remember when you called me amiga for the first time."

Manuela smiled and squeezed my hand. "Amiga, let's jump rope again!"

It is so nice to have a friend to confide in and one who helps you put aside your worries!

And I am blessed because my friendship with Francisco Chang is growing too. He and I like to sit together in his store at the end of the long counter while Juan Chang works at the other end.

Now that Francisco is used to me coming by, he has shown me more of his drawings. He's very talented and can sketch plants and flowers and trees in great detail. I told him about the ceiba tree that cries in Manuela's yard, and he said he'd like to draw it sometime.

"Do you believe a tree can cry?" I asked.

"Maybe," he said. "Everything is different in Cuba."

"But you like it here?"

"I like it a lot. The people are so friendly. I just wish they'd call me by my name, Francisco, and not always say 'chino' or 'chinito.' But I know they don't mean it badly—it's their custom."

"It's the same with me. Everyone calls me 'la polaquita.' In Poland, I wasn't even considered Polish. I was just a Jew. I had to come to Cuba to become Polish. It's funny, isn't it?"

We laughed, and Juan Chang turned from his accounting and said, "Esther, you should visit more often. I haven't heard Li Qiang laugh like that in a while."

I was suddenly confused. "Wait, so your name isn't really Francisco?"

"No, Francisco is my Cuban name. My real name is Li Qiang. But no one would be able to pronounce it here. At first it felt strange, but I've gotten used to being Francisco."

"I guess when we move to a new place, we become other people."

"I know. Sometimes I look in the mirror and ask, 'What happened to Li Qiang? Where has he gone?' But there's a piece of him still in me somewhere."

I knew just what he meant—I could barely remember the girl I'd been in Poland, working for Yoelke the baker, sweeping ashes and crumbs.

I turned to Francisco. "Do you want me to call you by your real name, Li Qiang? Did I say it correctly?"

"You said it right, Esther. But no, call me Francisco. That's who I am now."

His face grew sad. He waited until Juan Chang stepped out for a moment to add, "Also, Li Qiang means 'strong,' and I don't think I deserve the name."

"Why do you say that?"

He whispered, "Because I miss my family in China, especially my mother, who gave me my name. I cry at night on my pillow."

"Lo siento," I said, and thought about the tears I'd left on my pillow. Then I told him, "I cry too, but I don't think that makes us weak. We cry because there are people in the world we love so much that it hurts when they are far away. And how can you be weak when you were brave enough to come here on your own to help your uncle and your family back in China?"

Francisco smiled at me. "Perhaps you're right, Esther. I'm glad you know my real name."

"I will not forget that part of you," I told him. And in my heart, he'd always be a boy called Strong in Chinese.

With love forever,

Esther

AGRAMONTE

May 23, 1938

Dear Malka,

I felt a pang I'd never felt before when leaving Agramonte today. As the train full of strangers pulled out of the station, I missed Manuela and Francisco, I missed Señora Graciela and Doctor Pablo, I missed Juan Chang, I missed Ma Felipa and Mario José, and of course I always miss all of you. It seems like I spend a lot of time missing people!

But I was eager to arrive at Rifka Rubenstein's store and deliver the next batch of dresses and get more orders and keep saving to be able to pay for your steamship tickets. We walked in and Rifka Rubenstein's store was quiet. She sat behind the counter, leafing through the Yiddish newspaper.

She looked up and smiled. "Here you are, right on time. You are wonderful, Esther! Like a golden goose. The orders keep coming in."

She marveled over the new dresses. Then she noticed the label I had discretely sewed onto the back of the neckline.

"What is this? 'Designs by Esther'?" Rifka Rubenstein said. "Really, dear child, I think you have perhaps gone a little too far. You have an extraordinary talent, but putting a label on the dresses . . ."

I knew Papa wouldn't like it if I made a fuss, but I had to interrupt her.

"I am the creator of the dresses and I believe they should carry my name. Nobody has to know that Esther is a young refugee girl from Poland."

But Rifka Rubenstein wasn't happy. "I cannot accept the dresses with these labels. You will have to cut them out if you want me to sell them."

It was then that a sophisticated lady walked into the store. She wore a beige dress with a beige jacket and a belt cinched tightly at her waist. She carried a beige purse, no bigger than an envelope, in one hand and sunglasses in the other.

I knew Rifka Rubenstein would have liked for Papa and me to disappear, not to be standing at the counter with our sweaty faces and our dusty satchels. Papa bowed his head and stepped aside, trying his best to be invisible. But I stayed put. Rifka Rubenstein would have to pick me up and move me herself if she didn't want me there. Sure enough, glancing at Papa and me from the corner of her eye, she said, in her best Yiddish-accented Spanish, "My friends, you have made such a long trip to come visit me, maybe you'd like to rest in the back room while I take care of the lady?"

Before Papa or I could reply, the lady spoke. "I've heard from friends that there are some very well-designed dresses being sold here. Who, may I ask, is the designer?"

Rifka Rubenstein replied, "The designer is from New York."

"I know all the designers in New York. You see, I come from El Encanto. What is the designer's name?"

Rifka Rubenstein raised both eyebrows. "El Encanto?"

The sophisticated lady nodded. "I am Isabel de la Fuente, and I work at the salon de señoritas of El Encanto. I want to see if the dresses would be right for our young ladies. We choose only the most original designs at El Encanto."

I felt my entire body trembling at her words. Mutely, I picked up a dress and pointed to the label.

"What is this?" she said. "'Designs by Esther'? Who is Esther?"

In the clearest Spanish I could muster, I said, "Yo soy Esther."

"You are the designer?"

I nodded.

"And these dresses are made by you?"

I nodded again.

She turned to Rifka Rubenstein. "Is this true?"

Rifka Rubenstein sighed. "I cannot hide the truth anymore. The dresses are designed and sewn by this talented young girl you see standing here, who is accompanied by her father, Señor Abraham Levin."

"You have an air of someone from another part of the world. Where are you from, Esther?"

"I am polaca," I said. "But really I am judía." I used the

word "Jewish" rather than "Hebrew" so she would not think I was anything but what I am.

"None of that really matters to me. I want to see the dresses. May I look at them more closely?"

I passed her a batch of dresses that I had made for young girls and one for an adult woman. She examined them slowly and then turned to me. "These are beautiful and very original. I would like to take them to show to my boss at El Encanto. How much are they?"

Papa, who stood watching and barely breathing, suddenly said, "Please just take them and show them to your boss. We'll settle the price later."

Rifka Rubenstein gasped. She had not responded quickly enough and she was regretting it. I was so glad Papa had spoken for us.

But I had made the dresses for Rifka Rubenstein to sell in her store, and it would have been rude not to ask her for permission. In my sweetest voice, I said, "Would you mind if Señorita Isabel takes a few of the dresses to El Encanto?"

Trying not to seem annoyed, Rifka Rubenstein responded, "Of course I don't mind. Please take the dresses, señorita. It's thanks to me that this girl has been sewing since the day she arrived in Cuba!"

The lady looked at Papa and me with curiosity. "And where do you live? How will I find you?"

Papa smiled. "We live in Agramonte."

"Don't tell me! Isn't that somewhere in the countryside of Matanzas?"

"It's a little far, but we've gotten used to taking the train, and the people have been kind to us there."

Rifka Rubenstein couldn't stay quiet. "But you had your money stolen in Agramonte. How can you say the people have been kind to you there?"

"Most everyone is kind. There is only one bad pineapple," Papa responded, making a silly joke.

The lady laughed. "You are very gracioso," she said. "I am so glad I have met you and your talented daughter. It would be easiest if you both came to El Encanto in a few days. How about Thursday? What do you say?"

Papa and I smiled at each other.

"We will be delighted to come on Thursday," Papa said.

She replied, "I will be waiting for you." Then she took my dresses with her, dresses I had held next to my heart, and said adiós as she slipped out the door.

Rifka Rubenstein paid us for the rest of the dresses, and I was happy that she no longer seemed to mind about my label. Again, we put most of the money in her safe box.

"You are a lucky girl," Rifka Rubenstein said to me.

I remembered how Bubbe always feared the evil eye when someone gave her too big a compliment. "Pooh, pooh," she'd say to ward off the evil spirits. "Pooh, pooh," I whispered to myself. But come rain or shine, Papa and I would be at El Encanto on

Thursday. This time I would not allow anyone to make me feel like a fly being swatted away.

In the meantime, we agreed to make thirty more dresses for Rifka Rubenstein, plus an additional five dresses to make up for the ones we had given to Isabel de la Fuente. As usual, she gave us fabric and supplies to fulfill the orders she had taken—and some extra for myself.

The whole ride back to Agramonte, I could only think about the day we'd return to Havana and go to El Encanto.

And I kept saying "pooh, pooh." I was afraid to dream, afraid to be lucky.

With all the love a sister can
give another sister,
Esther

AGRAMONTE

May 26, 1938

Dear Malka,

Time seemed to pass much too slowly as I waited to go to El Encanto. I decided I must make a special dress for the visit. I pulled out some white cotton fabric that was soft like a handkerchief. I cut the cloth into the wraparound style that no one had worn yet except Manuela and me and added lace trim around the edge of the hem.

Finally the Thursday we had agreed upon arrived and we set off for Havana. Papa carried his empty satchel so we could bring back challah and a few other things. The trains were crowded as usual, and I sat stiffly with my arms on either side of my lap to protect my dress.

We arrived early, and Papa and I set off at a leisurely pace to El Encanto, winding our way through Havana's streets and plazas. As we passed by the Capitolio, its dome shimmering in the sun, one of the street photographers came up to us and asked if we wanted a picture. I assumed Papa would say no, as we never spend money on anything but essentials, but he asked the photographer to take a picture of me.

"You look nice in your white dress, my child, and it is such a beautiful day. We should remember it."

I stood in front of the Capitolio, and the photographer set his camera on its tripod and snapped the picture. After a few moments, he handed me a square of paper, still wet, bearing an image of me smiling into the camera. The first picture of me in Cuba.

I stared at the girl in the picture. Was this really me? Esther from Govorovo? I didn't recognize myself. I had changed in the last few months. I stood straighter; I was more sure of myself. And now I looked like I belonged here. The white dress caught the rays of Cuba's sunshine and it seemed as if I was glowing with happiness.

"Muy bonita," the photographer said. Then he added with a chuckle, "Hold the photo by the edges until it dries. That way it will last until you are old like me."

Papa and I continued on, and as we got closer to El Encanto, I began to feel nervous. But the guard who had told me to leave the last time now opened the door. We entered, and the store was all lit up and glittering, with glass counters filled with perfumes and powders.

We went up to a pretty woman wearing red lipstick who stood behind one of the counters and asked if she knew how to find Isabel de la Fuente.

"Is she expecting you?"

Papa nodded.

"She's on the fourth floor. You can take the elevator." She pointed to the end of the hall.

An elevator? What was that? Both Papa and I were too embarrassed to ask.

We went in the direction she pointed and saw people entering what looked like a steel closet. A woman dressed in a stylish suit with a lapel flower sat on a small stool. "Entra, entra," she said.

We squeezed in, along with many other people, and she pressed a lever. The contraption took us into the air. Even though I was standing still, it seemed like I was flying.

"Primer piso."

"Segundo piso."

"Tercer piso."

The elevator stopped on every floor and people poured in and out, some proudly holding shopping bags filled with the things they'd bought.

Finally I heard, "Cuarto piso."

Waiting there to greet us was Isabel de la Fuente with a big smile.

"¡Bienvenidos! ¿Cómo están, Señor Abraham y Señorita Esther?" She gazed at my dress and said, "How lovely you look, like a palomita."

I didn't mind being compared to a little dove.

How wonderful it felt being treated not like an annoying fly, but like an important person.

Isabel de la Fuente led us to the salon de señoritas, where they sold clothes for young girls.

Here, she said, was where they wanted to sell my dresses. Her boss thought my designs would be very popular with the girls and their mothers who shopped at El Encanto. But there was a problem. She lowered her voice to a whisper. She'd kept it a secret from her boss that I was a refugee. The law in Cuba didn't allow refugees to work. Also, I was too young. But Isabel de la Fuente had a suggestion. "Since your father is your guardian, and he is a legal resident in Cuba, we could name him in the contract. Is that all right with you, Esther?"

I tried to answer as best I could, with Papa helping me with some Spanish words.

I told her, "All the dresses I am making are for one reason—to bring my family here from Poland. My mother, my grandmother, my sister, and my three brothers are waiting for us to send them their steamship tickets. I will be happy to have the contract in my father's name."

"Muy bien," Isabel de la Fuente said. "Then we can work together. You won't have to sew all the dresses yourself anymore. We have a factory, and the dresses can be made there."

"A real factory with many workers and many sewing machines?"

"That's right," she said, and smiled.

"So what will I do?" I asked.

"You'll design the dresses, creating the samples for us, and then we will make them."

This was going to be so much easier than working for Rifka Rubenstein! I could still sew a few dresses each week for her, but now I'd be able to experiment with different designs and they'd make as many copies as they wanted for El Encanto.

When Isabel de la Fuente told us what we'd earn for the sale of the dresses, Papa and I hugged each other. We'd be earning triple what Rifka Rubenstein paid for each dress!

"If the dresses sell, we can pay you more," Isabel de la Fuente added, and I thought to myself, *Pooh, pooh, this is too good to be true.*

Isabel de la Fuente said they liked the designs of the dresses they had borrowed with the buttons down the front and the pockets at the hips and planned to make them in many sizes and fabrics. If we gave El Encanto permission, they would start sewing those right away in their factory.

Papa looked at me to be sure I agreed. Then he said yes and he read through the contract carefully before he signed it.

"Look, my dear Esther, see what it says here."

Papa smiled and pointed to the part that said the label on the dresses would read, "Designs by Esther. Exclusively for El Encanto."

"Is that all right with you?" Isabel de la Fuente asked me.

"¡Sí, sí!" I replied, almost fainting with joy.

"I had a good feeling this would all work out, so we prepared an advance for you," she said, holding out an envelope. "I am so pleased for you both."

Then Isabel de la Fuente praised my designs once more and

asked if I could come up with two or three new designs by the end of June.

Of course I said I would.

Everything seemed to glitter afterward, not just El Encanto, but the whole world. We stopped at Rifka Rubenstein's to deposit the money in her safe, and when Papa saw how much Isabel de la Fuente had given us, he exclaimed, "She is an angel God has sent to us. Now we'll take a stroll on the Malecón to celebrate. Remember, Esther, how you wanted to go for a stroll on the day you arrived in Havana and we didn't have time? Today, we make time!"

We crisscrossed through the crowded streets of Old Havana and found our way to the Paseo del Prado, an elegant boulevard lined with marble benches and shaded by a canopy of trees. Sculptures of lions stood regally on each corner.

"They say Havana is the Paris of the Caribbean," Papa remarked. "I doubt I'll ever get to visit Paris, but this seems like a very fine city to me."

"I don't know how Mama ever got the idea that Cuba was one big jungle. Papa, look at that mansion! It's like a frosted cake!" I pointed to a tall building with elaborate designs and a curly balcony on its third floor.

We both laughed and kept walking, feeling the sea pulling us forward.

Then there it was—the beautiful sea! And stretching around it, like a necklace, the seawall the Cubans call the Malecón.

We strolled along it, feeling the salty mist on our faces, enjoying the breeze.

"Be careful!" Papa yelled as I pulled myself up on top of the wall and dangled my feet over the side.

It was scary to be up so high, staring down at the wide blue sea. But I took a deep breath and felt a little braver.

I thought of you, Malka, and Mama and Bubbe and my brothers, how far you all still are from us. I wanted to stretch out my arms and give you a hug. But my sorrows were mixed with my joys. The sea was calm and peaceful and seemed to be whispering to me, *I will bring your family to you. Soon, soon, soon.*

Then I turned back around and said to Papa, "Thank you for the stroll on the Malecón. Now let's go home to Agramonte. I have many more dresses to make!"

Sending you all my love,
Esther

AGRAMONTE

June 14, 1938

Dear Malka,

We returned to Havana today, as I had finally finished making all the dresses I owed to Rifka Rubenstein. When we walked into her store, she complimented me for getting a contract for my designs with El Encanto, but also reminded me that she had seen my talent before anybody else.

"And I'm so grateful you gave me my start," I told her. "I can still make some dresses for your lady customers, if you'd like. How about thirty dresses a month? I'll sew a unique design for your store that they won't find at El Encanto!"

"You are a good girl, Esther. That is kind of you. I'm happy for your good luck, but don't let it go to your head. Remember you are a Jew and a refugee."

"I never forget. My sewing is to help my family. Thanks to my work for you and the designs for El Encanto, we're making money faster than we expected. We thought it might take years before we could even imagine being reunited again. Hopefully we will bring our family to this beautiful island soon!"

"Yes, let's hope that day comes quickly." Rifka Rubenstein sighed. "For some, Cuba is a paradise, but I don't want to be in the tropics forever. The sun gives me headaches and the humidity is turning my bones to mush. I want to be in New York, where I can wear a winter coat and mittens and the snow makes everything quiet. And if we stay here too long, we'll start to think we are Cuban and forget who we really are."

"But I want to be Cuban!" I exclaimed.

"A Jew can never be anything but a Jew."

"That's what Hitler and the Nazis want us to believe, but it's not true. We can be anything we want to be."

Oh, Malka, I truly believe this. On the train home, I thought about how much I've learned being a refugee in Cuba. And I've made the most wonderful friends. But I understood what Rifka Rubenstein was trying to say. I will not forget our Jewish customs and traditions, but that doesn't mean I can't learn about other ones, does it?

With all my love,

ESTHER

AGRAMONTE

June 23, 1938

Dear Malka,

Every time we visit Rifka Rubenstein, she gives Papa a stack of Yiddish newspapers from New York that she's finished with. Papa has spent days reading and rereading them. The news is getting more and more frightening, with such awful things happening to the Jews in Austria ever since the Nazis invaded. Papa read aloud stories about people being beaten in the streets and thrown out of their homes. I asked Papa if such terrible things could happen in Poland, and he said he hoped not, since so many Jews have lived there for a such long time. Every day Papa and I hope you are all safe.

And now, Malka, it pains me to tell you what has happened here.

We were just getting ready for bed a few nights ago when we heard knocking on the door. Papa cracked it open and Señor Eduardo pushed his way inside. He saw the Yiddish newspaper in Papa's hand and said, "Is that some secret alphabet only you people can understand? I bet that newspaper contains information that is a threat to Cuba. How did you get it?"

"A friend in Havana gave it to us," Papa replied.

"So you have friends in Havana? Why don't you go and live there? I see you coming and going on the train. Why have you come here? Did they send you here to spy on us?"

Papa said, "We are from a small town in Poland. We wanted to live in a small town in Cuba."

Señor Eduardo snickered. "My sister, Graciela, is a fool to let you rent this house for pennies. If it were up to me, you'd be in the street."

"What do you want from us?" Papa asked.

"Let me see what's in your pockets."

He moved closer to Papa, and Papa pulled out all the money in his pockets. It was a small amount to pay for the things we needed every day.

"That's all? Where's the rest?"

He raised his hand. He hit Papa and knocked him to the floor.

"No!" I screamed.

I went to the front door and opened it wide.

"¡Por favor! ¡Por favor! ¡Por favor!"

I didn't know how else to call for help. It was night and Calle Independencia was deserted. Then I caught sight of someone in the darkness—a man hurrying toward me. Fortunately, it was Mario José.

"Papa!" I said, and it was enough for him to understand.

He rushed into the house and helped Papa to his feet. Papa had a bump on his forehead and was dizzy. We sat him down in one of the rocking chairs and I sat next to him, whispering, "Papa, Papa, it will be all right."

"What have you done to this innocent man?" Mario José asked.

Señor Eduardo said, "Go now, Mario José. This is none of your business."

"You have hurt Señor Abraham and frightened Esther."

"I told you to leave. So get going."

"I am not leaving until you promise to stop attacking Señor Abraham and Esther. They're our neighbors and they deserve to be treated with respect."

"Neighbors? They are judíos who have come here to make money, to take away jobs from Cubans. The girl is making dresses to sell in Havana. It's against the law. She's a refugee. They should be arrested, father and daughter!"

"They aren't taking anything from anyone. They have come to Cuba because they can no longer live in the country they are from. All they want is to live in peace here and bring their family to be with them."

"Ask yourself, why aren't they wanted in their own country?"

"They have done you no wrong, yet you keep attacking them," Mario José said. "Stop bothering Señor Abraham and Esther, or I'm going to get the workers to call a strike!"

"Look, Mario José, you know I have nothing but respect for your mother, Ma Felipa. She saved my life when I was a boy.

I can't forget that. And you and I grew up together at the sugar mill. But you're a fool to let these foreigners come between us!"

Señor Eduardo stormed out, taking the money from Papa's pockets.

"Lo siento," Mario José said to both of us. He turned to Papa. "I'm going to tell Doctor Pablo to come over right away and have a look at you."

A few minutes later, Mario José returned with Doctor Pablo, who was upset too. He gave Papa a cold compress and made sure he was going to be all right.

At the door, before leaving, he said, "Señor Abraham, I am ashamed to be related to Señor Eduardo. My brother-in-law forgets that when José Martí fought for Cuba's independence, it was to create a nation where people of all backgrounds could live in harmony. That's the Cuba I believe in. Sleep well, Señor Abraham, and I will stop by in the morning to see how you're feeling."

And then the house was finally quiet, dear Malka, and we were grateful to feel safe again.

With love always,
your faithful
Esther

AGRAMONTE

June 24, 1938

Dear Malka,

You won't believe what happened today! This morning, Mario José and the workers called a strike at the sugar mill. And the workers all asked to join the Anti-Nazi Society of Agramonte.

Manuela came by early to see if I could come with her to the sugar mill to show our support for the strikers, and Papa said I could go. Then we went and got Francisco so the three of us could be together. We were eager to get there, and as we got farther away from Agramonte and were out in the open fields, we started racing one another just for fun. It wasn't long before we were sweaty and tired, so we stopped at the edge of a sugarcane field to rest.

"I had forgotten how fast I could run!" I said as I caught my breath.

"Me too!" Francisco said. "I don't get to run anymore since I'm always helping my uncle in the store."

Manuela nodded but didn't say anything. She looked downcast, and I wondered why she was suddenly so sad.

"Are you not feeling well?" I asked her.

Her gaze settled on the sugarcane fields surrounding us and she didn't say anything for a long while. At last she said, "As we were running, I thought of the people before me who were enslaved, how so many wished to run away to freedom. But most who tried were caught and punished with beatings. Only a few got away. They were able to live as free people, hiding in the woods, in palenques, as we call them. While running, I asked myself, Would I have been able to run to freedom? Could I have run fast enough?"

Her voice trailed off. Francisco and I drew closer, and we each took one of her hands and huddled together.

"It's horrible how there can be so much cruelty in the world that people have to run for their lives. Imagining what your abuela Ma Felipa went through is enough to make you lose all hope," I said. "At least those days are over, but the sugarcane workers are still not being treated right."

"I hope this strike helps," Francisco added.

"Yes," said Manuela. "I do hope it helps all of us."

We all felt ready to continue then and headed toward the mill.

As we walked, I gazed up at the clear blue sky and said a silent prayer of thanks that we were all free here.

Mario José had called for a peaceful strike, and the workers were gathered around the entrance to the mill when we arrived. Several held their machetes, waiting to go back to cutting the last of the cane so that it could be turned into molasses. I saw many friendly faces from the days when Papa and I peddled statues and sandals in the countryside.

The three of us quietly stood with Mario José, who held the keys to the mill in his hand.

Soon Señor Eduardo appeared, galloping in circles on his horse and raising dust. Pointing at me, he yelled, "This is all your fault!"

My heart beat fast. I was so afraid. But now Manuela and Francisco put their arms around me and I felt better.

Manuela whispered, "Don't listen to him. This strike is for every one of us. We're standing up against all his injustice."

Furiously looking down at the crowd from his horse, Señor Eduardo yelled to the workers, "You want to starve? That's fine! No work, no pay!"

He rode off and no one said a word as we all stood still under the scorching sun.

Then an old man called Agustín began to speak. He'd lost an arm feeding the cane into the rollers to squeeze out the sweet juice, but he was still one of the best sugarcane workers. He was famous in Agramonte for wielding the machete expertly with one arm.

"Let the sugar rot in the fields, if that's what he wants. Let him get a taste of the bitter suffering of our ancestors."

"Sí, sí, sí," people said in response, and they remained standing tall. Then they began murmuring among themselves.

"We won't give up," they said.

"He can't scare us anymore with his threats."

A little while later, Señor Eduardo returned and surprised

everyone by announcing, "All right, this is enough silliness. You'll all get a raise if you return to work in the morning."

Agustín raised his machete in the air and everyone cheered. And that was how the strike ended.

Later we heard that Señora Graciela had spoken to her brother and urged him to treat the workers more fairly—and for once he must have listened. Even though the strike only lasted one day, dear Malka, it was long enough to teach Señor Eduardo a lesson. He saw he needed to cooperate with Mario José and the workers if he wanted to keep his sugar mill running. And he told Mario José that he still couldn't stand the sight of Papa and me, but he'd leave us alone as long as we stayed out of his way.

I don't think I'll ever understand people like Señor Eduardo. His hatred is like a shard of glass in his eye that distorts his vision. But today I learned that when people band together, they can make things better for everyone. The sugarcane workers were willing to stand up for Papa and me, losing a day's pay when they earn so little. That was the most generous of gifts, and yet they shrugged when I said "Gracias" and simply answered, "De nada," as if it were the most natural thing to do. Tell me, Malka, why did I have to travel so far to find myself at home, here among the palm trees of Cuba?

With all my love as always,
Esther

AGRAMONTE

June 28, 1938

Dear Malka,

Isabel de la Fuente asked me to bring two or three designs for new dresses, but I got inspired and prepared four designs. Since I no longer had to sew multiple copies of the dresses, I had time to play around. I made a version of the wraparound dress with ruffles at the hem. For the dress with the buttons down the front, I made them with different collars and with different sizes of pockets in the front.

I folded the dresses neatly and Papa put them in his satchel. When we arrived in Havana, we confidently walked to El Encanto and didn't hesitate to enter. Papa and I weren't afraid of the elevator anymore! We went straight up to the fourth floor and found Isabel de la Fuente in the salon de señoritas.

"Buenos días," she said. "You have come at the perfect moment. We just put a few of the dresses we made from your designs on display."

She led us to a rack where the dresses hung from cushioned hangers. Then she pulled down a few dresses for me to see. There was the label she had promised: "Designs by Esther. Exclusively for El Encanto."

I looked at the dresses and couldn't believe how gorgeous they were! The fabrics were more luxurious than anything I ever could have imagined, some in fine cotton and some in silk. And the prices they were charging for the dresses! How could something I'd made with my own hands be worth so much money? I thought of Mama and how pleased she'd be. Then I felt sad. Only rich girls could afford the dresses I'd designed. But I consoled myself with the thought that the more money my dresses sold for, the quicker you would all come to Cuba.

"Did you bring new designs?" Isabel de la Fuente asked.

I nodded and she took us into an office filled with boxes of merchandise. There, I pulled out the sample dresses I had made.

She looked at them eagerly. "¡Divino! ¡Bellísimo!" she said as she examined each dress.

I had left the wraparound dresses for last. I pulled one out and showed her how easy it was to put on and tie around the waist.

"I love this style, like the white dress you wore last time."

I was so proud she remembered my white dress.

"This dress style is original and very flattering. It will be a wonderful addition to the collection." She smiled. "Next time you come, we will have these new designs on the rack."

She gave Papa a thick envelope with some money, then lowered her voice to a whisper. "Remember, we have to be careful. No one can ever know that a refugee girl designed these dresses. We would be in terrible trouble."

Papa responded, "No one knows."

"Very good," she replied. "There are secrets that we keep to do good in the world. And this is one of those secrets."

We said goodbye and headed to Rifka Rubenstein's to put our money in her safe box. It was a lot more money than the last time, and as usual, Papa left all of it behind except for the small amount we needed to survive from day to day. I gave Rifka Rubenstein ten of the thirty dresses I had made for her to sell in the store, and she was very pleased I was still loyal to her.

Then we hurried back to Agramonte. I went to sleep dreaming about my dresses, in silk and fine cotton, hanging on cushioned hangers, all of them with the label "Designs by Esther. Exclusively for El Encanto."

With all my love,

Esther

AGRAMONTE

July 19, 1938

Dear Malka,

Last month it was Shavuot, and Papa and I read the Book of Ruth. I read it again last night and thought a lot about it. When Ruth says, "Wherever you go, I shall go," that is how I feel being here in Cuba. I've come to a strange land and am now a part of it. With our friends standing up for us here, creating the Anti-Nazi Society of Agramonte, and leading the strike of the sugarcane workers, I know there is no returning to Poland for me ever again. I think I should have been named Ruth, not Esther!

I spend a lot of my time when it is raining or too muggy outside copying out the poems from the book *Simple Verses* by José Martí. This way, I am learning them better and may even figure out how to become a poet someday!

Whenever I hold the worn book, I remember it was once held in Emilia's hands, a girl who left the world too soon and will always be missed by her parents, Doctor Pablo and Señora Graciela.

How I wish I could write a poem for Emilia, telling her how she isn't forgotten!

How I wish I could write poems that express all my feelings—happy and sad and everything in between!

These letters I am saving for you, dear Malka, are the best I can do for the moment. And in writing them, I've discovered what a comfort it is to keep a record of my life so it doesn't feel like the days are blowing away in the wind and lost forever.

In the meantime, as my Spanish keeps improving, I marvel at the beautiful ways that José Martí says things. I have learned that for much of his life he lived in New York, not in Cuba, but he wrote in Spanish, not in English, just as I write in Yiddish, not in Spanish. I wonder if the first language you learn in life will always be the language of your deepest feelings, even if you learn other languages.

José Martí wrote many poems that are about poems, like this one:

¿Qué importa que este dolor
Seque el mar y nuble el cielo?
El verso, dulce consuelo,
Nace alado del dolor.

Who cares if this pain
Dries the ocean and dims the sky?
My verse, sweet consolation,
Is born from pain with wings.

What I know for sure is that these letters are born from pain with wings, because we are far away from each other. But these letters are also my sweet consolation as I wait for you and all my family to arrive.

From your sister, who wishes
she were a poet,
Esther

AGRAMONTE

August 7, 1938

Dear Malka,

Today, on Tisha B'Av, the saddest day of the year, Papa is fasting in memory of the tragedy that took place long ago, when the two Holy Temples in Jerusalem were destroyed. Those were the first temples of the Jewish people. After they were lost, everyone fled in different directions and ended up in many parts of the world. I wonder how our ancestors found their way to Poland? I imagine them crossing forests of cedar, dusty desert roads, and deep oceans, and eventually settling in Govorovo. I am sure they thought we would be in Poland forever, not imagining we would one day have to leave and try to create a new life in Cuba.

I heard an expression here in Agramonte that says, "El mundo da muchas vueltas." It means "The world spins round and round." The world is a carousel and you don't know where you'll end up.

Even though Papa spent the entire day at home praying, he let me work on my sewing. He said I was working too hard to be fasting, but I fasted along with him.

This is the time when the mangos ripen to a delicious sweetness. Mario José gave us several mangos from their fields, and in the afternoon, Papa said I should eat one. They looked so good and I was very hungry by then. But how could I bite into a sweet mango knowing Papa was fasting until nightfall?

When it got dark, Papa and I finally took a sip of water and sat down to eat the mangos together. They tasted sweeter because we waited to eat them.

One day you will taste this sweetness, dear Malka. I can't wait to see you bite into a mango! I warn you, mangos are messy—the juice gets all over your hands and drips down your chin—but it is worth it.

With all my love,
Esther

AGRAMONTE

August 18, 1938

Dear Malka,

One of Mama's ragged letters arrived today and we were so happy to hear from her after all these months. It was a short letter, and Papa read a few lines aloud to me because Mama began in such a surprising way—saying she missed me! *I realize now how much I took all of Esther's work for granted, how hard I was on her.*

Then Mama told Papa that if the money he sent for living expenses had arrived just a day later, you all would have had to go begging in the streets. Thank God it came when it did.

I know now why Papa doesn't let me read Mama's letters, because most of the news is not good, and now I've learned you've been going hungry. After fasting with Papa, I know a little about how that emptiness in the pit of the stomach feels. It hurts to think of you, my dear little sister, and my family suffering in this way, not just one day but many days. And my heart broke at the news that Mama had to sell her silver candlesticks to buy food. They were her most precious wedding gift. Those were the candlesticks she used each week to light the Shabbos candles.

When Papa was finished, he handed me the letter, and as I held it in my hands, I suddenly noticed that on the edge of the paper, hidden under Mama's signature, there was a note from you, Malka! Just a few words, but they gleamed like a thousand pieces of gold—"I love you, big sister, and send you a hug across the ocean. I hope you can feel it."

"Look, Papa!" I said. "From Malka!"

You should have seen the look of joy on Papa's face. And he said to me, "Hold on to this letter, dear Esther, so you will keep your sister close."

Yes, Malka, I do feel your hug and send you a hug back.

Always,
ESTHER

AGRAMONTE

August 29, 1938

Dear Malka,

When Papa and I got to El Encanto this morning, we acted like sophisticated people, calmly taking the elevator to the fourth floor. I was pleased with myself because I'd come up with another new design, a dress easy to slip on over your head, with no buttons down the front or ties at the waist. I liked the design so much, I made a dress for myself with leftover fabric and was wearing it for the first time. My sandals were worn and dusty, but my dress was new and fresh.

We found Isabel de la Fuente standing by the racks of dresses for young girls. She was wearing one of my dresses! It was the dress with the buttons down the front, which she'd carried off the day we met at Rifka Rubenstein's store.

She greeted us with her usual friendliness and pointed to the racks behind her. "Look, Esther, more of your designs! They're selling well. We're very pleased."

I wanted to run my hands over all the luxurious fabrics, but they weren't mine to touch.

"Come, let's talk in private," she said.

She led us inside the office, crowded as usual with boxes of merchandise, and handed Papa a thick envelope.

"I added a little extra money," she said to Papa. "I hope it helps you bring your family here." She turned to me with a twinkle in her eye. "Esther, I see you have a new dress on today. It looks so comfortable."

I showed her the sample I had made, just like the one I was wearing.

"This is wonderful, Esther! So practical and elegant! Perfect for our collection at El Encanto!" She smiled. But then she grew serious. "I am so sorry, Esther, but this will be the last of your designs that I will be able to sell at El Encanto."

"Why, what has happened?" I asked.

She explained, "I am moving to New York. I have an aunt who will take me in. I know it's a dream, but I want to find a job at one of the stores on Fifth Avenue. It won't be easy. I can barely speak English. But I have to give it a try." Then she whispered, "There's no one here I can trust with our secret. I don't want you and your father to get in trouble with the law."

I was so saddened by this news that all the words I knew in Yiddish, in Polish, and in Spanish drained out of me.

"Esther, I will always wear this dress that you made with great pride. I will show it off to everyone. I am sorry I couldn't do more for you."

Papa said, "Don't be sorry, Isabel. You have done so much for us."

"I did all I could," she responded. "Please come at the

end of October. I'll have another envelope ready with your earnings for the last sales of the dresses. Look for a very tall saleslady. She will give you the envelope."

She hugged me warmly, like an older sister, and said, "Let's not say goodbye. I hope we will meet again."

Then we went to see Rifka Rubenstein. We told her about Isabel de la Fuente's plans to move to New York and she said, "Esther, didn't I tell you it was too good to be true? I knew it couldn't last. How were they going to allow a Jewish refugee girl to design dresses for such an exclusive clientele? Be glad it ended quietly and no one is putting you on a boat back to Poland."

Before we left to return to Agramonte, I went to the back room with Papa to put away our earnings in the safe box. When he opened the envelope with the money that Isabel de la Fuente had given us, Papa was stunned. "She was very generous again. I tell you, my daughter, she was an angel in our path."

Malka, we are now so close to having what we need to buy the steamship tickets for all of you! I'll keep making dresses for Rifka Rubenstein, and when we get the next envelope from El Encanto, we will have enough!

With all my love,
ESTHER

AGRAMONTE

September 7, 1938

Dear Malka,

Papa was napping and I went to visit Manuela, thinking we'd jump rope and sing rhymes, but I learned it was an important holiday today in her religion.

A large crowd had formed at Ma Felipa's front door. The steady beat of the drums could be heard from the street.

Inside, I saw that everyone was dressed in blue and white. Mario José was playing the large batá drum and the other drummers followed his lead. Manuela had joined the women in the dancing. Ma Felipa was leading the singing.

I recognized the words I'd heard before:

Yemayá Asesu
Asesu Yemayá
Yemayá Olodo
Olodo Yemayá . . .

They were calling to the water, the water that flowed inside Ma Felipa's house from the fountain that never dries.

They were calling to the sea, the water I had crossed on a ship, the water that separates me from you, dear Malka.

They were calling to the water that falls from our eyes when we're sad, the water we call tears.

Maybe I hadn't cried enough about everything I'd lost, everything I was scared of in this world, and that was why the tears started coming.

I had a puddle of tears at my feet.

But that couldn't be true. Who can cry that much?

All I know is that I was crying and crying and I had an urge to run and see if the ceiba tree was crying too.

I went outside. There was the ceiba tree with the chain wrapped around its trunk from the days of slavery in Cuba and the white flowers tucked into the chain.

When I got closer, I saw them clearly, big wet tears falling from the top of the tree down the bark.

The tree was crying and I was crying.

I didn't know if I was awake or dreaming.

Then I felt many arms holding me up. Manuela and Ma Felipa and several very old women, thin as twigs, were making sure I didn't fall to the ground. They said to me in a cooing voice, "Ya, ya, ya." There, there, there.

Soon the tears stopped streaming down my cheeks and the ceiba tree stopped crying too. They brought out a chair and sat me down.

When I came back to myself, Manuela was standing next

to me. "You felt it, Esther? How the power of the drums can sweep you away?"

I nodded, not yet able to speak.

Then the drums stopped playing, and the singing ended.

People were milling around, talking to each other. Manuela said it was the cumpleaños of Yemayá. Her birthday. She said Yemayá wanted to talk to me, that was why I cried so much. My tears made the ceiba tree cry.

It felt as if I'd been there for many hours, but it wasn't so long. When I went back to Papa, he'd just woken up and was sitting in a rocking chair, lost in thought.

How could I tell him what happened? Would he believe Yemayá wanted to talk to me and that's why I cried and the ceiba tree cried with me?

I thought it better not to tell him. I didn't want him to think I was wavering in my faith as a Jew.

What I can't tell Papa, I tell you, dear Malka. You are my sister and you will understand me.

With all my love,
ESTHER

AGRAMONTE

September 26, 1938

Dear Malka,

Even from this great distance, I want to wish you a happy Rosh Hashanah and good health in the New Year. Singing "Avinu Malkeinu" with Papa, I thought of you and Mama and Bubbe, Moshe, Eliezer, and Chaim, and realized almost eight months have passed since I arrived here, so far from my family. I am fortunate to be with Papa, and you are fortunate to be with Mama and Bubbe and our brothers. But it is unfair that we are not all together, and thinking about this makes me sad.

Papa says not to be sad today, because if we are sad on the first day of our New Year, the whole year will be sad.

He said we should each say a prayer in our own way, and if we really meant it, then God would hear it. I had only one prayer in my heart: *Next year may we all be together in Cuba.*

Afterward, Papa and I ate rice with a fried egg, as we always do for dinner.

A gentle knock on the door surprised us.

It was Francisco. He bowed politely to Papa.

"I brought you something for your New Year celebration," he said.

"How did you know?" I asked.

"My uncle told me. He was in Havana the other day, at the port, waiting for his merchandise. A few hebreos were waiting for their merchandise and they told him that today is your New Year. My uncle asked what special foods you eat on this day, and they gave him this."

He held out a cardboard box tied with a string. The label on the box said it was from Goldstein's Bakery in New York. Inside was an apple strudel.

Papa and I were thrilled. An apple strudel in Agramonte! No apples grow in Cuba, so this was very special!

We thanked Francisco for the marvelous gift. Papa asked him to stay and have a slice of strudel with us, but he said he had to help his uncle in the store.

Francisco reached into his pocket and pulled out another gift. It was a tin of the Polish sour cherry tea. "My uncle thought you might like more tea."

And he turned and slipped away into the night.

The strudel was delicious. Rather than leave any of it to be eaten by the ants while we slept, we ate it all, down to the last crumb.

I went to bed thinking what a special New Year celebration it had been, thanks to Juan and Francisco Chang's gift. They had understood about our New Year because they too have a different New Year. Francisco told me that in the Chinese calendar, it was the Year of the Tiger, when anger can become courage.

Hearing that made me feel hopeful, Malka. I remembered how the sugarcane workers had used their anger to fight against injustice, and if we can all use our anger to make the world a little bit better, that would be such a good thing!

Your sister, who always
remembers you,
Esther

AGRAMONTE

October 5, 1938

Dear Malka,

Since Yom Kippur is the holiest day of the year, Rifka Rubenstein had insisted we come to Havana and stay overnight with her and go pray at her synagogue.

Papa told me that morning that I could just fast for half the day, but I decided to fast for the whole day along with him and Rifka Rubenstein. I'd fasted once before and knew I could do it again.

When we arrived at Rifka Rubenstein's house, a big pot of chicken soup with kreplach and a honey cake greeted us, but we had to wait—we'd only get to indulge after an entire day of prayer and hunger.

And what a long day it was!

But it was amazing to be surrounded by so many other Jewish people, all of them praying and singing and greeting us like old friends, even when we were meeting for the first time.

"It's the Day of Atonement," whispered Rifka Rubenstein. I sat next to her in the women's section, upstairs from where Papa sat with the men. "I have some smelling salts, if either of us grows faint. It isn't easy to fast, but we must do it. We have come to ask for forgiveness today."

I'd heard about asking for forgiveness before, but still wasn't sure what that really meant.

"All of us have come to ask for forgiveness?" I asked Rifka Rubenstein.

"Yes, all of us Jews. We ask God to forgive us."

"What have we done wrong?"

"Listen to the prayers, Esther. Read what it says in the mahzor."

I listened to the many things we have done wrong.

We have been faithless.
We have been presumptuous.
We have spoken falsely.
We have gone astray.
We have let our hearts grow hard.

I watched as Rifka Rubenstein tapped her chest with her fist as she prayed. I turned to each side of me and saw all the women doing the same. Then I looked below at the men and they were tapping their chests with devotion too.

It was beautiful to see how sincerely they prayed. I wished I were better at praying. But I recited the words along with everyone.

And then, after a while, the words weren't just words anymore, Malka.

I began to feel them deep inside me, like the beating of my heart in my chest. Bubbe and those who came before, and before, and before, had recited these very same words and tapped on their chests.

As the words moved through me, they shone a light on my life. Maybe my heart had grown hard and I hadn't realized it? But by praying and asking for forgiveness, I could make my heart soft again so it could fill up with love.

Suddenly I understood that there were people whose hearts had turned to stone. Their hearts had become so hard, they had no room for love, only for hate.

At last nightfall came. The sound of the shofar woke me from my thoughts. *Tekiah, Shevarim, Teruah, Tekiah Gedolah.*

Then the fast was over and we ate Rifka Rubenstein's delicious chicken soup with kreplach and sweet honey cake. I was grateful not to be hungry anymore. And after a whole day of asking myself how I could try to be a better person, I felt a little less afraid of all the scary things going on in the world.

With all my love as always,

ESTHER

AGRAMONTE

October 25, 1938

Dear Malka,

Our day started out sad, knowing Papa and I were going to El Encanto for the last time. We took the elevator to the fourth floor, and the first thing I noticed was that my dresses were gone. The new dresses now on display looked starched and formal, and none of them had pockets!

We went over to a very tall saleswoman in rickety high heels.

"Buenos días," I said.

The saleswoman knew who I was from my accent. "¿Eres Esther?" she asked. "¿La polaquita?"

I nodded and she motioned for us to follow her. She led us into the office where we had always met with Isabel de la Fuente. Once the door was closed and the three of us were alone, the saleswoman passed Papa a very thick envelope. Papa placed it at the bottom of his satchel, where it would be safe.

We both felt sorry about the loss of Isabel de la Fuente in our lives, and took a long, meandering walk through El Parque de la Amistad, the sprawling park filled with palm trees behind El Capitolio. Young couples in love and mothers with small children lingered on benches, munching on peanuts and enjoying shaved ices with sugary syrup, whiling away the time. It was such a beautiful sunny day in Havana, it seemed like nothing could be wrong in the world.

We walked past the park and ended up in a neighborhood we'd never seen before, a part of the city where Chinese people lived. Restaurant tables covered in bright red tablecloths spilled onto the street. I could smell the jasmine from the Chinese food, which I so much wanted to taste. Papa would never let me eat it because it contained pork.

As we walked along a street called Zanja, we came across a peddler selling newspapers in Chinese.

"Papa, let's get a newspaper for Francisco Chang."

"Of course," Papa said. "That will be a nice gift for your friend."

We went to see Rifka Rubenstein afterward, and she had big news.

"I received my visa to go to America, the real America!" she announced. "My turn comes in two months, so I will leave Cuba in December."

"Congratulations," Papa said. "Your wish has come true."

"Yes, finally." Rifka Rubenstein sighed. "But I have much to do in the next two months to get ready."

"Can we help you?" Papa asked.

Rifka Rubenstein smiled. "Would you like to manage the store after I leave?"

"What a surprise!" Papa responded. "I thought you'd want help packing up to go to New York."

"I can pack my own bags, thank you. But I will need money to get settled in New York. That's why I don't want to sell the store. If you'll manage it for me, we can split the profits half and half. That way, you'll earn money and so will I."

"I can't think of a more perfect arrangement," Papa said.

Rifka Rubenstein looked pleased. "You and Esther can live upstairs in my apartment, and there's plenty of room for your family too when they come."

My head started spinning. I closed my eyes and opened them again to make sure I wasn't dreaming.

Then Papa said, "I'd be glad to manage the store. Esther and I will live upstairs and prepare everything for the arrival of our family from Poland."

Suddenly I imagined myself in Havana. It would be exciting to wake up to the cries of the peanut vendors, the hustle and bustle of people rushing from place to place, the honking cars, the smell of coffee and fragrant tobacco smoke from the cafeteria across the street. But I'd no longer hear crickets and birds bursting into song in the morning and the roosters crowing. I'd be far from my friends, Manuela and Francisco Chang, and the weeping ceiba tree, and Yemayá's water that pours from the ground inside Ma Felipa's house. A gloom settled over me as I thought about everything I'd miss from Agramonte.

Rifka Rubenstein frowned. "You're so quiet, Esther. Cat got your tongue?"

I shook my head, unable to speak. "I don't know, I—I'm sorry," I stammered.

"My, oh my! You are a strange one, Esther," Rifka Rubenstein replied. "You should be jumping for joy. You'll finally get out of the countryside and come to the city. You'll be able to meet other Jewish children and go to a Jewish school."

I tried to smile. I felt a lump in my throat.

Papa understood. He put his hand on my shoulder. "My child, don't be sad. You'll have time to say goodbye to Agramonte. We have two months still to go."

"That's right, it's not as if you're moving tomorrow," Rifka Rubenstein said, a touch of sympathy in her voice. "Think of how much you'll enjoy helping your papa in the store when you come home from school. You can sell your dresses here as you did at the beginning. If you want to put anything else on the labels, be my guest. I won't care anymore, since I'll be in New York!"

We went to the back room and Papa opened up the envelope Isabel de la Fuente had left for us. "The angel was kind to us again," he said. "How will we repay such kindness?" Then Papa counted all the money we had in the safe box.

"We have almost enough now!" Papa said happily. "Next time we come to Havana, we'll get the steamship tickets and send everything else they'll need for the journey." But then Papa became sad. "It's all thanks to you, Esther. I couldn't have raised the money alone. You've seen what a terrible salesman I am."

"Papa, we've done it together. But you say we need a little more money?"

"Yes, we have enough for their tickets and visas, but we need extra to make sure they don't run short during their journey. It's harder to leave Poland now. They are making it more and more difficult for Jews to come here. Many palms have to be greased."

"What does that mean, Papa?"

"People like Señor Eduardo, every step of the way, demanding money. If you don't pay them, they will block the path."

"I am going to make lots more dresses so we can sell them here in the store. With each stitch, I'll bring Malka and all of our dear family closer to us."

Papa smiled. "Wonderful, my child. What a blessing your sewing is."

We filled up our satchels with fabric from Rifka Rubenstein's store. Then we stopped at Zvi Mandelbaum's store to pay him the commission we still owed him from the sale of the sandals on the installment plan.

"You have done so well!" Zvi Mandelbaum said when he saw us. "Do you want more sandals?"

Papa shook his head. "Not at this moment, but maybe when my sons come, we will go peddling."

"Your sons? Are they on their way to Cuba? That is wonderful news! At last your family will all be together!" Zvi Mandelbaum said, smiling at Papa and me.

"They are not on the way yet. How I wish they were. But we have raised almost all the money we need for their journey," Papa replied.

Zvi Mandelbaum raised his eyebrows and looked at us with curiosity. "Well, I know you haven't made a fortune from peddling."

"It's Esther. She has magical hands," Papa told him.

"I can sew, that's all," I said. "I am fortunate that my mother taught me, and now we can sell my dresses."

"That is truly a blessing!" Zvi Mandelbaum said, and he gave Papa a hug, practically lifting him off the floor!

We got on the train, and there was still a little light in the sky when we returned to Agramonte. I was glad to see the town again; it felt like home.

After I put away the fabric and washed up, I asked, "Papa, may I bring the Chinese newspaper to Francisco Chang?"

"You can, Esther, but be back before it's dark."

I rushed off and found Francisco at the counter, sketching in his notebook.

I held out the gift of the newspaper. "Un regalo," I said.

His eyes lit up when he saw the Chinese characters.

I told him Papa and I wandered behind El Capitolio and that's when we discovered the streets where Chinese people lived. He said he had heard there was a Chinese neighborhood in Havana and hoped one day to go there with his uncle.

I wasn't ready to tell him I'd be moving to Havana in two months.

I turned to leave. It was getting dark outside. Then Francisco opened his notebook and pulled out a sketch.

I stared at it, amazed at what it was. Francisco had drawn an aleph, the first letter of the Hebrew alphabet. He had made the aleph the size of an entire page and filled it in with colorful flowers and glowing stars.

He smiled. "I saw this letter in the newspaper at your house," he said. "It's a beautiful letter, so I thought I would draw it."

"Gracias, Francisco, muchas, muchas, muchas gracias."

We both laughed at how I said "muchas" three times. Then I rushed down the street with the aleph in my hand. When I got to our front door, I folded the drawing and put it in the pocket of my dress. This would be another one of my special memories from Agramonte, this gift Francisco gave me on the day I learned I'd be moving to Havana.

I'll always share my special memories with you, dear Malka. Very soon I will whisper them to you before we go to sleep, the way we used to share stories with each other in the dark of night when Poland was still my home.

With all my love,
Esther

AGRAMONTE

November 10, 1938

Dear Malka,

This morning while Papa was praying, I was busy sewing dresses to sell, but I was already imagining the dress I wanted to sew for you, Malka, in a sea-green fabric, like the color of your eyes.

We heard a loud knock on the door, too loud to ignore. I stood next to Papa as he took a deep breath before opening it. We feared Señor Eduardo was the one knocking. But it was Doctor Pablo.

His hands shook as he held up a Spanish newspaper. "Muy malas noticias." Very bad news.

"Please sit down," Papa said, pointing to one of the rocking chairs.

"I cannot sit. We must take action."

"What has happened?" Papa asked.

"Last night, the Nazis in Germany destroyed everything they could destroy that belongs to the Hebrew people. They smashed the windows of temples, of schools and stores. There is broken glass littering the streets. They are calling it the 'Night of Broken Glass.' Munich looks as if it's been bombed.

Many Hebrews have been killed. They have been ordered to turn in the keys to their houses and leave Germany. Those who have passports are fleeing. The ones who have nowhere to go are scared of what will happen next."

"Oh no, no, no, no," Papa said in a voice full of pain.

"Señor Abraham, get your family to Cuba. Hurry before it's too late." He pointed to the newspaper, and Papa and I stared at it in horror. The word *Jude* was scrawled on a store that had been ransacked.

Doctor Pablo said, "My dear friends, we must do everything possible to stop the Nazis from bringing their hatred to Cuba. The Anti-Nazi Society of Agramonte needs to organize a march. We must call attention to what is happening to the Hebrews and make sure the hatred in Germany doesn't cross the ocean and reach us. We don't have any poisonous snakes on this beautiful island. And we're not going to allow that Nazi venom to take root here."

He rushed off and spoke to Ma Felipa, Mario José, and Manuela, as well as to Juan and Francisco Chang. They fanned out all around Agramonte, sharing the news of the Night of Broken Glass and the rally being organized to keep the Nazis from coming to Cuba.

By the end of the day, men, women, and children filled the main street, Calle Independencia. Some were from the center of town and some from the hamlets nearby, from the huts and barracks that Papa and I got to know as we walked around with our heavy satchels hanging from our shoulders. The sugarcane workers called out to me, "¡Polaquita, aquí estamos!" Little Polish girl, here we are! It was sweet to hear those words. They didn't understand the difference between Polish and Jewish, but it didn't matter; they wanted to show they cared about us and thought we belonged in Cuba as much as anyone else.

Señora Graciela came and stood next to us. She was wearing the dress I'd made for her and whispered in my ear, "As you can see, I love this dress, Esther."

"I want to make you another, Señora Graciela. But I don't have black fabric. Could I use fabric that is a dark blue?"

"Dark blue will be fine, Esther. I'll never forget my beloved Emilia, but I've grieved so long for her, I think she wants me to put aside my mourning clothes and feel a bit of happiness again."

As my eyes filled with tears, Señora Graciela pulled out a freshly ironed handkerchief from her dress pocket and said, "Keep it. Let it be a souvenir."

I remembered the handkerchief Bubbe had given me and that I'd given to the man named Jacob before I got on the train to Rotterdam. Had he made it across the ocean? Had he been reunited with his family? So many people are looking for a place to call home. I want to imagine that the world has a very large heart and can give all of us who have lost our homes a chance to start over.

Ma Felipa came with Manuela and they hugged me with so

much warmth, I wanted to melt. They pointed to Mario José, who was sitting on a bench with two other men, each with a batá drum on their lap.

"The drums are to call the spirits and the ancestors," Manuela whispered. "We need their strength to protect us from the Nazis."

Francisco and Juan Chang arrived with a banner. Francisco had made it. In neat handwriting, he'd written in Spanish: LA SOCIEDAD DE AGRAMONTE EN CONTRA DE LOS NAZIS. On the four corners of the banner were Chinese characters.

"What do they mean?" I asked.

"They stand for faith, peace, love, and hope," Francisco said.

"They're beautiful," I told him.

"I'm glad you like them, Esther," he said with a smile.

Doctor Pablo came and grabbed Papa by the elbow. "Come on, we'll start walking and everyone will follow."

They set off down the street, and Mario José and the other drummers sounded the drums, softly at first and then with more force.

Manuela stood to my left and Francisco to my right. Between the three of us, we held up the banner as we walked behind Doctor Pablo and Papa.

Señora Graciela took Ma Felipa's elbow, Ma Felipa took Juan Chang's elbow, and they followed after us.

The crowd came next, moving to the beat of the drums.

Several people added their own sounds to the music. Some clapped together wooden sticks known as "claves." Some rattled maracas. Some scraped güiros made from polished gourds. And some banged on pots and pans. At the end of the line were Mario José and the two other drummers, playing their drums as they walked.

The march came to a stop on a clear patch of land at the edge of town. A makeshift stage had been created out of a few wooden planks. Doctor Pablo climbed up and everyone, even the babies, quieted down to listen.

Doctor Pablo began, "The Anti-Nazi Society of Agramonte thanks you for coming tonight to this rally. We are here to say we have no animosity toward the Hebrews who have come to Cuba searching for a new home."

People clapped. Then someone said, "Let him talk! He's not finished yet."

Doctor Pablo continued, "It isn't easy to be a refugee. It isn't easy to find your way in a new place and learn a new language. No one leaves their country unless they must. The Hebrews are suffering now in the lands where they have lived for centuries. That is why they are escaping and looking for a new home in Cuba. Señor Abraham and his daughter Esther became our neighbors, and they've won our affection and respect. We're here to tell them they're safe on our island. We won't allow a Night of Broken Glass to happen in Cuba. Some of us believe in God. Some of us believe in African spirits. Some of us believe in kindness. Whatever you believe, we come together to say no to the Nazis in Cuba!"

People cheered and sang out, "Nazis, no, Nazis, no, Nazis, no! No, no, no!"

Then the drummers came to the stage and resumed playing. Ma Felipa led several women in a slow dance, swaying back and forth, while others milled around saying hello to each other. Little children chased after one another, playing tag, and then got in line when a man came selling shaved ices with different sugary syrups.

"This is Cuba," Doctor Pablo said, laughing. "We can only be serious for the briefest moment. Then there's a party, an all-night pachanga."

"But we accomplished our goal," Juan Chang said. "That's what matters."

"We're so grateful to all of you," Papa said. "Esther and I were lucky to come to Agramonte."

"You will have a home here always," Señora Graciela said.

I was sadder than ever that we would soon be leaving Agramonte.

A gentle breeze blew and no one seemed in a rush to go to sleep. The hurricane season was over. We had been spared the harsh winds that made autumn an uncertain time of year. Everyone was glad to gather and enjoy the night as the moon rose in the sky and the stars shone bright.

Then all of a sudden we heard the sound of a horse galloping. My body began to shiver and my teeth chattered.

Francisco was the first to notice and came next to me to say, “Esther, it will be all right! We're here with you.”

But I still had a terrible feeling when Señor Eduardo rode over to us, sitting high on his horse.

“Who gave permission for all these people to assemble here tonight?” he said, gazing at Doctor Pablo.

Doctor Pablo replied, “No permission was needed. This is a peaceful gathering of the Anti-Nazi Society of Agramonte.”

“¿Qué dice?”

“You heard what I said. We are taking a stand against the Nazis and their discrimination against the Hebrews.”

“That's ridiculous! The Nazis are doing the right thing in Germany. That's why I'm proud we now have a Cuban Nazi Party and I can be with them.” He glared at Papa and me. “How much longer do we have to put up with these people invading our country? If it were up to me, I'd have them pack their bags right now.”

Señora Graciela came closer. “Please, Eduardo, you mustn't speak that way. Señor Abraham and his daughter Esther are good neighbors, and we want them to feel at home in Agramonte.”

Ma Felipa put her arm around my shoulders. Manuela, Francisco and Juan Chang, Doctor Pablo, and Señora Graciela formed a circle around Papa and me. Mario José put down his drum and joined the circle too.

“It's best you go now, Eduardo. The night began in peace and we want it to end in peace,” Ma Felipa said.

Señor Eduardo cowered before Ma Felipa. Without saying another word, he rode away on his horse, leaving a cloud of dust. Everyone cheered. And the drumming and dancing went on until dawn.

With all my love,
Esther

AGRAMONTE

November 11, 1938

Dear Malka,

I barely slept after staying up so late last night. And once asleep, I had a nightmare about the Nazis storming into Govorovo with torches and setting the town ablaze. You and Mama and Bubbe and Moshe, Chaim, and Eliezer were running for your lives. I stretched out my arm and it turned into a thick rope. "Grab hold of me!" I yelled, and I pulled and pulled, trying to steer you toward me, toward Cuba. Then Señor Eduardo appeared on his horse and I had the terrible thought that I would fail to bring all of you here.

In the morning I was still scared from the nightmare, but I set to work on a dress for Señora Graciela in the dark blue fabric. Knowing that Señora Graciela is Señor Eduardo's sister and yet so different from him, I calmed myself as I stitched together her dress. I used the wraparound design with a wide collar and one large front pocket so it would be another style from the dress I made for her in black.

I sewed all day and finished it, and Papa let me bring the

dress to Señora Graciela. She was delighted and put it on right away, tying the bow at her waist and twirling around. "This was the dress I needed! Emilia's favorite color was blue! I'm sure my beloved daughter is glad I can remember the happy days we shared."

I gazed at the painting of Emilia in the living room and wished I could bring her back into the world for even a second so they could hug each other again.

Señora Graciela took my hand and we sat down on the sofa. "Esther, I want to apologize again for my brother, Eduardo. But as you saw last night, all of us support you and your father. You'll always have a home here in Agramonte."

I should have told her then that we were moving to Havana, but I couldn't bear to. I wasn't ready to say goodbye.

I know our move will give us more opportunities and enable us to spend time with other Jews. But I have come to love the people of Agramonte, and if I had to stay here, I feel I could live among them joyfully for the rest of my life and still be Jewish. As the poet José Martí has taught me, I come from many places. Agramonte will always be my first home in Cuba.

Dear Malka, the time is getting close when you will be coming to this place—Papa and I are going to buy your steamship tickets tomorrow! Then we will read these letters together and you'll know everything about my life in Cuba while I waited for you. Until then, I run my finger along the sweet words you wrote to me at the bottom of Mama's letter and I feel you close.

With all my love as always,
Esther

AGRAMONTE

November 14, 1938

Dear Malka,

I can hardly describe how excited Papa and I were to finally be going to the travel office to buy your steamship tickets! But first we had to stop at Rifka Rubenstein's store to pick up the money in the safe box. When we arrived, she sat in her usual spot behind the counter, waiting for customers, reading the Yiddish newspaper.

"Have you heard about the Night of Broken Glass?" she asked as we walked in.

Papa nodded. "We have heard. It is very disturbing news."

I quickly added, "But we have very kind neighbors in Agramonte. They organized a rally. They want to keep the Nazis out of Cuba."

"Don't tell me your neighbors did that? They are not even Jewish!"

"There are good people in Cuba who want to help us, and it doesn't matter if they are Jewish or not!"

"Oh my, Esther, dear child, you are so innocent. You think they care what happens to us?"

"Yes, they do! We have friends in Agramonte who have

welcomed us. We can't go around thinking everyone hates us! How will we ever live in this world?"

Rifka Rubenstein shook her head. "Some people hate us and there is nothing we can do to change that."

Papa listened, not saying a word. He finally said, "Both of you are right. There are good people and hateful people—and indifferent people, neither good nor hateful, just waiting to be told how they should think and feel."

"Those are wise words, Avrum, spoken like the scholar you are," Rifka Rubenstein said.

"Thank you," Papa said. He sighed and went on. "Frightening things are happening in the old country, but today is a joyous day for us. We finally have enough to buy the steamship tickets for our family. Let's hope we can find a better future here in Cuba. And you, dear Rifka, may you be blessed and find a better future up north with your beloved family."

"That is very kind of you, Avrum."

Rifka Rubenstein turned and gave me a hug, surprising me. "I may speak harshly to you, Esther, but you know I love you like my own granddaughter."

Papa and I took our money from the safe box, split it in half, and put it in our two satchels.

"Don't act as if you are carrying lots of money or the thieves will smell your fear," Rifka Rubenstein said. "Here, take these remaindered rolls of fabric and stuff them into your satchels so you'll look like you're peddling."

We followed her advice and went off to the travel office, walking side by side, except when the streets grew narrow or people rushed past us. Havana never felt so crowded. Every time I took a step, I bumped into someone. I held on to my satchel tightly and Papa did the same. Imagine if we lost our savings after so much hard work and months of dreaming of being together here in Cuba!

Fortunately, we arrived at the travel office with our satchels intact. But there were many people ahead of us. They sat in rows in the steamy room, eyes half closed, looking as if they'd been waiting for hours.

Someone said, "Get a number and sit down. They'll call you."

We sat and waited. It seemed to take forever.

At last they called our number. We jumped up and rushed to the desk of the woman who would attend to us. She wore her black hair in a long braid and had a weary expression. She tried to smile as she asked, "How may I help you?"

"We need six steamship tickets from Poland to Cuba for the earliest date you have available," Papa said.

"Are these tickets for your family?" she asked.

Papa told her, "Yes, they are. They are for my wife, my mother, and my four remaining children."

She shook her head and her braid wiggled down her back.

"I must be honest with you, señor. It will be a long and difficult journey. And it will cost a lot of money. The travel company is forcing us to charge an extra amount in case any of the passengers aren't allowed into Cuba and have to be sent back on the same ship they came on."

When she told us the price for the steamship tickets with all the other expenses, I thought Papa would cry. He turned to me and said, "We are a little short of the total. We will have to come back another day when we have more money."

I whispered back, "Don't worry, Papa, I have an idea."

I told the lady we'd be back shortly with all the money, and she said to come directly to her when we had it.

We left the travel office, and I told Papa I'd sell my pocket watch to Zvi Mandelbaum.

"I don't want you to sell it," Papa said. "You received that watch as a gift."

"But I want to sell it," I told Papa. "Please let me."

Zvi Mandelbaum greeted us with his usual exuberance.

"Hello, my friends from the countryside. What brings you to the great metropolis of Havana today?"

Papa got right to the point. "We are a little short of money for the steamship tickets for our family, and Esther has a pocket watch she wants to sell to you. What can you give her for it?"

I knew Zvi Mandelbaum was a good businessman, so I wasn't expecting he would offer much.

"My, oh my, it's real gold," he said, astounded.

He offered a large sum of money, enough to cover the remaining expenses for your trip, with lots of money left over for our move to Havana. We'd be able to buy beds for the apartment. We'd have everything ready for when you all arrived.

I handed over the watch and Papa secured the money in his satchel. He stepped out the door, and as I was about to follow, Zvi Mandelbaum called to me. "Esther, come back, shayna maideleh. I have something for you."

Papa waited outside while I returned inside, expecting Zvi Mandelbaum to give me a candy or a trinket from his store. Instead, he held out the pocket watch.

He whispered, "Dear child, I have seen how hard you've worked with your father ever since you arrived in Cuba, how dedicated you are to reuniting your family. Take this watch back. It's an expensive watch. You may need it down the road for an emergency. Keep the money I gave you. May your family come to Cuba soon."

"Are you sure about this, Mr. Mandelbaum?" I dared to ask.

"I am sure. After the Night of Broken Glass in Germany, things will get worse for the Jews. We must help one another in every way we can. And I promise I'll give everyone in your family a pair of sandals as soon as they arrive!" He put the watch in my hand and said, "Don't tell your father. He's a proud man. He shouldn't think he owes me anything. Here's a key chain. Tell him I gave you that."

I thanked him for his kindness and put the watch back in my pocket. I showed Papa the key chain and he didn't suspect anything. He'll never know Zvi Mandelbaum could be so generous.

We returned to the travel office and the woman with the long braid was ready for us.

"While you were gone, I think we found you the best itinerary. Your family should travel on the *Orduña* steamship. I don't recommend they pass through Germany now. It is very dangerous. They will have to go through France."

She knew we were Jews, without having asked, because it was only Jews who came to Cuba from Poland.

She went on, "The *Orduña* is a British ship. It's part of the Pacific Steam Navigation Company. It boards at the port of La Rochelle in France."

"How will my family get to France?" Papa asked.

"They will have to sail from Gdynia in Poland to Le Havre in France. Gdynia is a few hours' distance from Warsaw."

She pronounced *Gdynia* in a funny way, with a Spanish accent, but Papa and I understood. We were too embarrassed to tell her we'd never traveled that far when we lived in Poland. Even going from Govorovo to Warsaw was a rare trip.

Then she continued, "From La Havre, they will have to figure out how to get to La Rochelle so they can board the *Orduña*. The ship will take them to Liverpool and Bermuda and will make a stop here in Cuba."

"Is there no other route they can take?" Papa asked.

"I assure you this is the safest route. The *Orduña* is one of the most reliable ships coming to Cuba right now. I have tickets available for January 16, 1939, in exactly two months. It seems like a long time from now, but they will need to get from place to place. They will need a medical examination. We have to get their visas too. There is much to be done."

We opened our satchels and took out the money we had saved. Papa added up the bills and paid the woman for the steamship tickets and the visas. The tickets will be wired to Poland. Papa is also wiring the money needed for all your other expenses.

In just two months, you will all be here, dear Malka! I wish the journey were easier, but the good thing is you will all come together. The boys can carry the suitcases. You and Mama can take care of Bubbe and be sure she doesn't get too tired. It will be cold in January, so you will need to bundle up with coats and blankets. But when you get to Cuba, you will toss away your woolen garments and let the sun warm your bones and gladden your heart.

I can't wait to see you and Mama and Bubbe and Moshe and Eliezer and Chaim arrive at the port of Havana! The distance of all these months, the sewing and the saving, will have been worth it just to say, "Welcome, dear sister, welcome to Cuba."

With love from your sister, who
is impatiently waiting for you!
ESTHER

AGRAMONTE

December 10, 1938

Dear Malka,

Today a telegram came from Mama telling Papa the steamship tickets and money for the journey had arrived, and we both breathed a sigh of relief. Now your trip here is beginning to feel real.

I said to Papa, "Think how proud Mama will be when she sees the store in Havana and our apartment upstairs with an indoor toilet. Did you tell her we're going to manage Rifka Rubenstein's store?"

"No, I didn't. I want to surprise her."

"She will be surprised! And happy. Our whole family will be!"

That night we had our usual rice with fried eggs for dinner. While we ate, I asked, "When are we moving to Havana?"

"In nine days," Papa replied. "We will leave Agramonte early in the morning so we can arrive to Havana in time to say goodbye to Rifka Rubenstein and pick up the keys to the store and the apartment."

"Nine days is very soon," I said. "I haven't told anyone we are leaving."

"You must start to say goodbye," Papa replied.

I knew Papa was right, but I wasn't sure how I would start. How do you say goodbye to all the people who have been kind to you in a new land?

Then I had an idea.

"Papa, next Saturday is the first night of Hanukkah. Can I invite our friends to come light the first candle with us?"

"My daughter, you make me smile how you are always thinking of ways to share our Jewish holidays with those who know nothing about them. But yes, invite them, why not? And then on Monday, we'll take the train to Havana and start a new life, counting the days until our whole family is here."

I went and invited Doctor Pablo and Señora Graciela, and then Francisco and Juan Chang, and they immediately said yes. Then I went and invited Ma Felipa, Mario José, and Manuela. They too said yes right away, and I stayed to visit with Manuela. I was sad I'd soon be saying goodbye to her but couldn't bear to tell her yet that we were leaving for Havana. It felt terrible keeping that secret from her. The afternoon was breezy, the birds were chirping happily, and the air smelled sweet from the guava and cane sugar that Ma Felipa had boiled in a big pot over an open fire to make squares of candied guava paste. I will miss my life here so much!

Manuela and I jumped rope, singing the rhymes together, letting the words rise into the sweet air. Finally, we got tired and ate thick slices of bread topped with Ma Felipa's fresh guava paste that tasted so delicious. I looked over at Manuela and wondered if I'd ever have a friend as kind and caring as her again. I reached into my pocket and wrapped my hand around the smooth object I'd been carrying around with me for so long. I realized at that moment that I was ready to pass it on.

"Can I tell you something, Manuela?"

"Tell me, Esther. Is something wrong?"

"I have to tell you that all these months that I've been in Agramonte, I've been missing my sister, Malka, in Poland. It's like a part of me is missing. I couldn't have survived without your friendship."

"And you've been a perfect friend to me, Esther, as close to a sister as I'll ever have. I'm glad you came to live in Agramonte."

I pulled out my gold watch. "Keep this watch, Manuela. Maybe you can sell it so you can go to school and become a schoolteacher, as you have dreamed."

"How can I take this watch from you? Don't you need it? I know how hard you've been working to make money for your family."

"They are on their way now, Manuela. Can you believe it? I hardly can. And now I want to pass this along to you. Just promise me you'll go to school."

"I will," she said. "Gracias, Esther."

We hugged and I ran back home to Papa. Then I sat down to write this letter to you, listening to the crickets singing and the palm trees swaying in the wind—it sounds like they are whispering goodbye, goodbye.

I imagine you are getting ready to say goodbye to everything that is familiar in Poland, to the wooden house where our family has lived forever, to the pale sky and the snowy streets. It is painful to say goodbye, but sometimes there is no choice but to close a door in hopes of another door opening.

With all my love as always,
Esther

AGRAMONTE

December 17, 1938

Dear Malka,

Just before sunset, our friends came over—Manuela, Ma Felipa and Mario José, Francisco and Juan Chang, and Doctor Pablo and Señora Graciela.

Everyone took their same places around our wooden kitchen table, and Doctor Pablo said, "You bring us all together whenever there is a Hebrew holiday. Tell me, is this another holiday where you deprive yourselves of eating bread?"

Papa laughed. "This holiday is different. Now we eat potato pancakes. Esther has made them with the sweet potatoes of this land. And we light candles, one each night for eight nights. We say thank you for the light that shines in times of darkness. Tonight we light the first candle."

"As you know, I don't practice any religion. I am a proud atheist," Doctor Pablo replied. "But a holiday where you light candles and say thank you that there is light . . . that seems like a good holiday."

We don't have a menorah here, but Papa was so clever! He took nine empty soda bottles and arranged four on one side and four on another side, with the tallest bottle in the center. Then he topped each bottle with a candle.

Papa said the prayer, and I asked Manuela and Francisco to put their hands over mine so we could light the first candle together.

Then I served the latkes. I told everyone to eat them with lots of sugar so they'd taste better. Oh, Malka, I don't think I'll ever be good in the kitchen. I beat the eggs and the oil, and Papa had to help me peel and grate the potatoes. The pancakes came out lumpy and uneven, not in nice round circles like Mama's. I guess I will need some lessons when you are all here!

"Delicioso," Señora Graciela said, pouring another spoonful of sugar on her pancakes.

Everyone agreed they were delicious. It's because they like sweet foods in Cuba. Between the sweet potatoes and the dark brown sugar on top, they were the sweetest potato pancakes I'd ever eaten.

After all that sweetness, I knew it would be painful to break the news of our move to Havana.

I cleared the plates and then blurted it out. "Nos vamos."

We're leaving.

"Where are you going?" Manuela asked.

"To Havana," I replied.

"But don't you like it here?" Manuela had a hurt look on her face.

"We love it here, but we have to move because my father

got a job in Havana. We're very sad to leave Agramonte. But the good news is that our family is coming from Poland in a month! We'll all be together at last in Havana."

"Of course we are happy for you but sad for us," Ma Felipa said. "We thought you were staying here forever. We've grown used to having you and your father as our neighbors."

Señora Graciela pulled out a handkerchief from the pocket of the new blue dress I had made for her. "It makes me want to cry. When will we see you again?"

Doctor Pablo spoke next. "Señor Abraham and Esther will be missed by all of us. But let's be reasonable. They are not moving far away. The trains go back and forth every day to Havana."

A silence fell over the room, and finally Juan Chang spoke. "We mustn't think of ourselves. If moving to Havana is the road Señor Abraham and Esther need to take, we should not stand in their way. Let us be glad our paths crossed in Agramonte and wish them well."

I was so grateful for all their kindness and love and wished I could think of the right words to say. Then I remembered the beautiful lines from José Martí and recited them aloud—

Yo vengo de todas partes,
Y hacia todas partes voy . . .

I come from many places,
And to every place I go . . .

Doctor Pablo laughed. "Our polaquita Esther knows she can always win us over with the words of José Martí."

The night had fallen like a soft blanket of darkness. From a distance, we heard the sound of the drums, and Ma Felipa stood. "I must go now. Tonight is the birthday of San Lázaro. We also call him Babalú-Ayé. Even though he's a beggar, he's a powerful saint who brings those who are ill back to health. The celebration is just beginning, but it will go on until late, with drums, dancing, and singing. You are all welcome to come."

I expected Papa would refuse to go and wouldn't let me go either. But he surprised me. "We will go," he said to Ma Felipa.

Her face lit up and she said, "¡Qué bueno!"

Juan Chang said that he and Francisco would also go.

And then Señora Graciela said, "We are invited?"

"Of course you are," Mario José replied. "Come along, Señora Graciela, and you too, Doctor Pablo. It's about time you danced at a bembé!"

We stepped out together into the night. The sound of the drums felt like a glowing light, shining as bright as the first Hanukkah candle. We followed the sound until we got to the yard near Ma Felipa's where the crowd had gathered.

Mario José started playing his drum and Ma Felipa began to sing. Manuela took Francisco and me inside the casa templo, the saint's house, to see the altar. "That's San Lázaro. Babalú-Ayé is his African name," she said, pointing to the life-size wooden statue. He had wounds on his legs and leaned on crutches. A purple cape was draped around his shoulders and a dog stood on either side of him. Glowing candles, bowls of beans, a plate of roasted corn, and coconuts were arranged under the statue. Manuela explained, "Even though he's a spirit, he gets hungry too and has to eat just like people do. But he only eats the aromas of what we offer him, and that gives him the strength to do good for us and take care of us."

When we went back outside, people were dancing. Some were dressed in burlap sacks like beggars and had purple scarves on their heads to honor the spirit known by his two names, San Lázaro and Babalú-Ayé.

Papa was standing together with Juan Chang, Señora Graciela, and Doctor Pablo. They were moving back and forth with the music, trying to fit in with the people around them.

I hooked my arm around Papa's arm and whispered, "It was nice of you to come tonight."

"I didn't know it would be so beautiful."

The two of us swayed to the music along with our Agramonte friends, who looked at us and smiled.

Then Papa turned to me and said, "Just as we have carried the religion of our ancestors wherever we have gone, so have they whose ancestors came from Africa. I am glad I have seen with my own eyes the love with which they remember those who came before."

I never thought I'd hear those words come out of Papa's mouth. But Cuba has changed him too, as it has changed me, in more ways than I can say.

With all my love,
from your sleepless sister,
Esther

HAVANA

December 19, 1938

Dear Malka,

At the crack of dawn, the man that Papa hired to move our things to Havana arrived with his truck. He took the beds and linens, the table and the rocking chairs, and the sewing machine too. Señora Graciela insisted I keep it so I could continue making dresses. Within minutes, our little home in Agramonte was emptied of Papa and me.

While Papa said his morning prayers, I stepped outside to take a last look at our street in Agramonte. There was Francisco Chang bringing a gift wrapped in tissue paper.

"For you," he said. "Open it."

I pulled away the tissue paper, and inside was a rounded teacup. I held it carefully. It was made of porcelain and decorated with flowers and flying birds.

"I brought it from China," he said.

"I don't want to take it away from you."

"I have another one. You keep this teacup and I'll keep the other. When you drink tea in Havana, I'll be drinking tea in Agramonte."

Then he gave me another tin of sour cherry tea.

"Here's a little more tea," he said with a smile, and passed the gift to me.

I thanked him, and he nodded and said, "Buena suerte."

He wished me good luck because neither of us wanted to say goodbye.

When I went back inside, Papa had finished saying his prayers. We got our satchels and caught the direct train to Havana. Papa dozed off, but I was wide awake, gazing at the palm trees touching the sky and the sugarcane fields and feeling this is now my land.

Rifka Rubenstein was waiting with her suitcases, sitting behind the counter and reading the Yiddish newspaper as if it were an ordinary day.

"If you had arrived a minute later, I would have grown impatient, but you came at just the right time," Rifka Rubenstein said by way of greeting.

"Do you leave soon?" Papa asked.

"In fifteen minutes," she replied. "Here are the keys to the store and here are the keys to the apartment. Avrum, when you run out of fabric, I will send more from New York. Esther, remember to water the plants on the balcony." She smiled at us. "May your family arrive safely to Havana."

"Thank you, Rifka. May you arrive safely to New York, and may your family come soon so you can all be together," Papa said.

She turned to me. "Esther, since I think of you as like my

granddaughter, I took the liberty of going to the school and enrolling you. Classes are in Yiddish and Spanish, and you can begin in January. As my going-away gift, I have paid for the first term. You will meet other Jewish girls and boys. Finally you will be with your own people. Won't that be good?"

I thought of the Chinese teacup Francisco had given me, still wrapped in tissue paper in my satchel. I thought of Manuela telling me that the power of the African drums can sweep you away. I would never have met Francisco or Manuela if Papa and I had come straight to Havana and only been among Jews. I would have lived in Cuba without really knowing Cuba.

Rifka Rubenstein sighed. "Esther, you haven't answered me."

"Sorry, I was thinking. Thank you, that was nice of you to enroll me at the school," I told her, trying to sound enthusiastic.

"You will be glad I did," she answered. "Your papa too."

"We are very grateful to you, Rifka," Papa said. "Go in peace and don't worry about a thing. We will take good care of your store. And if there's ever anything you should want from Cuba, like a sweet pineapple or a juicy mango or a strong coffee, please tell us and we'll find a way to send it to you in New York!"

"I might take you up on that!" she replied, laughing.

We hugged, and a friendly driver arrived to help her with

her suitcases, carrying them all in one hand and extending the other to her politely so she could step down from the curb.

It was hard to believe that Rifka Rubenstein was going to the port to catch her ship to New York. Will she find happiness there? I hope so.

We waved to her from the front door and she looked back at us with tears in her eyes. Even though she'd been eager to leave Cuba, it seemed she would miss it more than she dared to admit.

Papa and I were unsure what to do next. We looked at each other like two orphans. The store and the apartment were now ours, so long as we did well and made enough for us to live on and for Rifka Rubenstein to earn a profit too.

We spent the day getting the store in order, arranging the fabrics by type and color. I hung a few of my dresses in the window again. Then the man arrived with the truck from Agramonte and we moved our things upstairs to the apartment.

I remembered to water the plants on the balcony. Afterward, I stood and watched our new neighbors taking down the laundry that had dried on the clothesline. I smiled and they smiled back. Farther away, I watched the streetlamps turn on at nightfall.

The city of Havana glowed as if lit by thousands of fireflies. Drivers honked their horns and people shouted and laughed as they walked on the street below. There was a bittersweet smell from the coffee brewing in the cafeteria on the corner.

I wondered why my lips tasted salty and realized it was from the sea. We are very near the harbor. Near the sea! This means we are near the ships. Soon you will be on one of those ships, dear Malka. I am closer to you here in Havana.

With immense love
from your sister,
Esther

HAVANA

January 8, 1939

Dear Malka,

It is 1939 already. You will all be here soon!

I have started school. I'm not as behind in my studies as I thought I'd be. My Yiddish hasn't suffered thanks to all the letters I've been writing for you in my best Yiddish. While I understand Spanish very well now, I haven't learned to write it. But Spanish is a generous tongue to newcomers. You write it the way it sounds, so it shouldn't take long for me to improve. And math comes easy to me after all the days of peddling and adding sums with Papa.

At first my classmates treated me as if I'd been living in the jungle for the past year. They didn't understand why I hadn't gone to school. They asked if I spent my days hanging from the trees eating bananas. They finally stopped teasing me when I told them about Señor Eduardo and how there are Nazis even in Cuba. Many have family back in Europe that they worry about and wish could come to Cuba. I told them about you, Malka, and about Mama and Bubbe and our brothers, and that you are on your way.

I hope I will make friends eventually, but right now I

just want to help Papa get everything ready for all of you. After school each day, I go back to the store and work with Papa, helping him sell the fabric. We sold a lot at the end of December. Women bought fabric to make special clothes for New Year's Eve and for Three Kings' Day, which is celebrated on January 6, with gifts for the children. Now sales have dwindled a bit, but Papa says that sales always pick up when I'm around. I make more of an effort to sell the fabric, showing customers everything we have in stock and giving them ideas about sewing.

My dresses have sold out, which is good, but I have to find time to make more. I only have the evenings and Sundays free, since we keep the store open on Saturdays, which Papa doesn't like, but we can't afford to lose all the customers who like to shop that day. We close a little early on Friday, which is "el día de los pobres," the day the poor go around to the stores in the old part of Havana asking for charity. Everyone gives them one penny, but I give them each two pennies. We get a challah, and Papa and I say the blessing, and then Papa goes to synagogue. He doesn't insist I go with him, and that makes me love Papa even more.

While he's at religious services, I wait for him on the seawall of the Malecón next to the port where the ships dock. I watch people disembark, imagining the day you'll be one of them. I love feeling the sea breeze on my face and seeing my dress flutter in the wind. Couples, young and old, sit close to one another on top of the wall. Fishermen throw their lines far into the ocean. Passing musicians strum old Cuban melodies on their guitars.

The sky is dark, but the first stars are very bright when Papa comes to meet me after he's done praying. We slowly make our way back to our new home in Havana, floating like in a dream.

Waiting anxiously to see you,
ESTHER

HAVANA

January 16, 1939

Dear Malka,

Today you should all be on board the *Orduña*. Papa has not received any news from Mama, so we hope you made it and are doing well.

We went to the travel office early this morning and spoke to the woman with the long braid who sold us the steamship tickets, but she said she isn't allowed to share information about the passengers.

"The *Orduña* will arrive ten days from now in Havana," she told us. Then she added, "Ten days . . . unless anything unexpected happens at sea."

She crossed herself and that scared me.

Then she looked around nervously. After making sure no one was listening, she whispered to us, "I shouldn't tell you this, but it's in the newspapers." She pointed to an article in the *Diario de la Marina*. "There are rumors the government is going to close the door to Hebrew refugees. They think there are too many refugees and they're taking jobs away from Cubans."

Papa said, "But you sold us the steamship tickets."

"We're selling steamship tickets to anybody who wants to buy them. We're salespeople. We just hope that the government will let everyone who has a ticket and a visa enter the island."

Oh, Malka, how our hearts sunk to hear this. We've worked so hard to bring you all to Cuba, to be reunited as a family. And now, was it possible that the hatred has settled here and that you might arrive at the port and not be allowed in?

The woman with the long braid looked at me with pity. "I am very sorry, señorita. As I said, these are just rumors. Let's not start worrying yet. Let's pray your family makes a safe journey."

Papa and I left the travel office so sad that neither of us could speak.

In the evening, before I sat down to write this letter, I listened intently to Papa's prayers and told myself I was going to have to pray more too.

With all my love,
ESTHER

HAVANA

January 22, 1939

Dear Malka,

These are the prayers that come to my lips and I whisper them to myself.

I pray the sea is calm and you are not seasick.

I pray that every now and then there is a smile on Mama's face and she becomes filled with hope for the new beginning awaiting her in Cuba.

I pray Bubbe knows how eagerly Papa, her only child, waits for her. Just like a little boy.

I pray Moshe, Eliezer, and Chaim are behaving and not fighting with one another and being kind to you. It's not easy to be the only sister. When you're here, there will be two of us!

I pray you will soon gaze at the seagulls flying over the beaches of the Caribbean islands surrounded by the turquoise sea.

I pray you will come to love Cuba and its people as much as I do.

I pray the distance that has kept us apart melts away the moment we meet again.

I pray we will meet again.

With all my love,

Esther

HAVANA

January 26, 1939

Dear Malka,

This letter is not what I expected to be writing on the day that your ship finally arrived. I thought we'd hug and kiss and our lives would go on. But our lives are a mystery, Malka. As much as we try to control everything, sometimes all we can do is pray . . .

It was still dark when Papa and I went to wait for all of you at the port at Triscornia. I held a bouquet of fragrant white gardenias as we stood outside the building through which you and the other immigrants must pass. There was already a crowd and everyone was nervous. We watched, like one set of eyes, as the *Orduña* crossed the harbor of Havana and dropped anchor. Papa clasped his prayer book against his heart. All of us had the same prayer on our lips—*Please, please, let them disembark.*

Then the health inspectors went on board. And we waited.

The sun rose in the sky. Soon it got unbearably hot. We were hungry and thirsty, but none of us moved, not willing to risk losing our precious spots near the entrance.

Slowly passengers began to trickle from the ship and into

the immigration building. We all searched desperately for a glimpse of our loved ones amid the swarms of people in their heavy woolen clothing and shoes. Shouts of joy broke the silence whenever someone exclaimed that they'd caught sight of a relative. I looked and looked, but it was far away and I couldn't see any of you.

Papa and I waited and waited.

We stood there until the sun slipped into the sea and the night came. Then someone in the crowd announced that no one would be released from Triscornia until the next day.

You can imagine with what sadness we went home.

On the ferry back to Havana, I carried the white gardenias I'd not been able to give you. As we crossed the sea, I saw the shrine to the Virgin of Regla and remembered she was also Yemayá and the sea was her home. Malka, in that moment, I could hear the drums from Agramonte calling to Yemayá, asking for help. I glanced at Papa and saw him with his eyes closed and lips moving silently as he said his Jewish prayers. I couldn't lose hope. I'd worked so hard and with so much love to bring you all to Cuba.

Now I am awake in the middle of the night, writing to you, and I wonder if my efforts have been in vain.

Hope—where have you gone?

Hope—have you flown away?

From your despairing sister,

Esther

HAVANA

January 27, 1939

Dear Malka,

Papa and I barely slept, and at the crack of dawn, we returned to the port. I carried the white gardenias to give to you, though they'd lost their sweet fragrance.

Suddenly, we heard a boy's voice yell, "Papa!"

It was Moshe. He rushed into Papa's arms. Then he smiled and widened his eyes at me and said, "You're all grown up! You're showing your arms and legs!"

"We're in Cuba, Moshe. Impossible to be covered up like in Poland!"

Eliezer and Chaim came next, also yelling, "Papa! Papa!" and hugged him with such force, I feared they'd crush him.

At last Mama came. She looked tired and there were dark circles under her eyes.

"Mama!" I yelled, and ran up to her.

"Esther!" she said to me with a pained smile, and I saw that my beautiful blue-eyed mother was missing a front tooth.

She collapsed into my arms and started crying. Papa came over and held her in his arms, but she kept on crying.

"Avrumaleh, Avrumaleh," she said, using her nickname for Papa.

She was crying from happiness, but she was also crying from sadness.

"Where is Bubbe?" I asked. "Where is Malka?"

Moshe and Eliezer and Chaim bowed their heads and stood around us in a circle. They waited for Mama to give the answer.

"Bubbe didn't come with us. She stayed in Govorovo," Mama said.

Papa let out a wail. Gasping for breath, he asked, "My mother? My dear sweet mother isn't here?"

"No, Avrumaleh, she isn't here. She said she was too tired and old to make such a long journey. Just getting to the ship was going to wear her out. A trip across the ocean to Cuba would surely kill her. And how could she go to Cuba and abandon the graves of her mother and father in Govorovo? She refused to leave her home. She gave us her blessing. She told me to tell you to forgive her. She hopes one day we will all return to Poland and be reunited there."

Tears slid down Papa's cheeks and Mama hugged him. "I am sorry, Avrumaleh, I am sorry," she said.

I stood there in silence with Moshe and Eliezer and Chaim, tasting the bitterness of the salt in the sea mist.

Then Mama went on, "Malka was miserable on the ship. She couldn't stop worrying about Bubbe and was seasick the whole journey. She barely ate and most of what she did she threw up. They've called a special doctor to determine whether she will be allowed to stay. Hopefully they'll finish the examination soon. If she's too ill, they may send her back."

Malka, dear Malka, it broke my heart to hear Mama say those words. But I understood how much it hurt you to leave our beautiful Bubbe, who has lived with us since we were born. I don't want you to feel like you have to carry alone all the sadness of the world we needed to leave behind. We are here for you!

Papa took Mama by the elbow. "Let's not lose faith. Malka is a young and sensitive girl. She feels things deeply, she is in pain, but she will recover."

And so we all continued to wait for you, dear Malka.

"Do you want me to take some of you home to rest for a few hours and return later?" Papa asked.

But after the long separation, none of us wanted to be apart again.

It was the middle of the afternoon, the hottest time of the day, when the streets become deserted as people rush home to rest in darkened rooms or sit in outdoor cafeterias drinking tall glasses of cool coconut water under awnings that offer the blessing of shade. Papa got us some cold sodas and we found a spot where the sun wasn't so bright. There, Papa and Mama, Moshe, Eliezer, Chaim, and I stood looking out at the ocean silently, a family missing two of its limbs, wishing for a bit of happiness.

Then a girl who looked like you came slowly toward us,

watching her every step as if there was quicksand underneath that could pull her to the center of the earth and swallow her whole. This girl was thinner and frailer than the Malka I remembered. Her woolen dress hung on her like a potato sack and she looked like she'd forgotten how to laugh. She wore glasses too big for her face. And I realized it was you, dear Malka, it was you!

You fell into my arms like a sparrow with broken wings.

"Esther, I missed you."

That was all you had the strength to say in a whisper of Yiddish.

You could barely clasp the bouquet of gardenias.

"Let's go to your new home," Papa said. He put his arm around you and looked at you, Malka, with such love in his eyes. "Now you will rest, my child, and soon you will feel better."

After we got off the ferry in Havana, we waded through the thick heat of the streets. Mama leaned against Papa with each step she took. She was twice his size, but he held her up. Moshe, Eliezer, and Chaim carried the suitcases. I led the way, pointing out the potholes so no one would trip and fall, never letting go of your hand, dear Malka, because I feared if I did, you would disappear like a ghost.

We turned off the Plaza Vieja and headed up Calle Muralla. There we bumped into Zvi Mandelbaum.

"The family has arrived! Mazel tov!" he said.

"Thank you," Papa replied. "They have had such a long journey, but we will visit with you another time."

We smiled at Zvi Mandelbaum and kept walking briskly, relieved to not have to explain that we were missing Bubbe, our dearest, sweetest grandmother.

My heart beat fast as we turned the corner and arrived at Calle Sol, the street of our new home. I was happy we'd live on a street called "Sun." I hoped for sunny days ahead for all of us.

Papa stopped in front of the building and said to Mama, "Here, downstairs, is our store, dear Hannah, and upstairs is the apartment where we will live." He unlocked the door to the store and Mama peeked inside. I could tell Papa was eagerly waiting to see what Mama would say. She began to smile and immediately put her hand to her mouth to cover it because of her missing front tooth. But we could hear the happiness in her voice as she said, "It's marvelous! So many fabrics! And in all the colors of the rainbow!"

Then we climbed the stairs to the apartment, Moshe, Eliezer, and Chaim racing to the top and the rest of us following behind. Papa opened the door and all of us kissed the mezuzah for good luck before stepping inside. Papa and I had swept and mopped and dusted the apartment from top to bottom, and the wooden furniture gleamed in the golden rays of the late-afternoon sunshine. Again, dear Papa stood close to Mama, waiting to see what she'd say. She looked around, then said, "I feared I was traveling to a jungle. But Havana is a pretty city, and this house feels like it could be a home for all of us one day."

Papa beamed with joy and said, "Oh, my Hannah, it will be!"

Moshe, Eliezer, and Chaim found their room and excitedly jumped from bed to bed. When I showed you ours, you noticed there were three beds there too. "Let's not touch Bubbe's bed," you said. "Maybe she will change her mind and come to Cuba soon."

"That's what we'll do, Malka," I responded.

And I showed you our common rooms—the kitchen and the sitting room with the two rocking chairs, from where you'll catch the sea breeze off the small but beautiful balcony and see Havana arise at dawn and go to sleep at night.

"I have been taking care of the plants on the balcony. Aren't they the greenest green? Look at how the orchids enjoy basking in their little square of sunshine!"

You looked, but you couldn't see yet; you were too worn from the journey.

"Malka, as I promised, I've been writing letters to you this entire year that we've been apart. We will sit side by side in the rocking chairs and read them together while the sea breeze keeps us cool. Won't that be fun?"

"Maybe in a few days, big sister," you whispered. Then you excused yourself and went straight to sleep.

Oh, dear Malka, your body has arrived in Cuba, but your heart is still with Bubbe in Govorovo. I trust we can help you feel better soon. In the meantime, I will keep writing letters to you as if you are far away, little sister, because it feels that way. And because, after writing so many letters to you all these months while waiting for you to arrive, writing has become a necessity for me—like water, like air, like sunshine. Writing to you has helped and comforted me. It has kept me alive.

Once you get better, I'll give these letters to you. They are for you and only for you. But I won't stop writing. I will start keeping a journal—and I will get you one too! You're carrying so much sadness, my sister, and I hope that if you can let the paper hold even a bit of it, you will feel better.

With all my love as always,
Esther

HAVANA

February 2, 1939

Dear Malka,

The most wonderful thing has happened today while you slept—Mama told me how proud she was of me. When I showed her the dresses I'd made with Señora Graciela's sewing machine, she was surprised I could sew so well. And when I gave her a dress I'd sewn for her, soft and flowing, with a pattern of little flowers and buttons down the front, her face lit up. She ran to the bedroom and came back wearing it.

"Esther, my daughter, this dress is so comfortable! You put my thimble to good use. You even learned to sew on a machine. All those times I was showing you how to sew, I didn't think you were paying any attention. But it turns out you were!"

Then she kissed my forehead and said how happy she was about all that I'd accomplished. It was the first time I felt loved by Mama and not just tolerated.

"I hope you will come to love Cuba one day, Mama," I told her. "And that you will no longer be angry with Papa and me."

"I decided on the boat here that I can't be angry anymore. I am no longer angry at you. But I am angry that the world has put us in this horrible situation. Most of all, I'm scared for Bubbe and for so many people back home."

"I know, Mama. There is so much evil in the world. But there are good people here, Mama. Most Cubans are so nice and eager to be friends."

"I hope so, Esther, I hope so." She pointed to the open balcony, from where the light streamed into the room. "I have to say that this warm sunshine in the middle of winter is very soothing."

She smiled at me again, quickly covering her mouth out of embarrassment.

"Mama, what happened to your tooth?"

"That terrible day when Bubbe announced she wouldn't travel with us, I was carrying a load of firewood and I tripped and fell and broke off my front tooth. I feel I've aged a hundred years."

"Don't worry, Mama. We'll go to a dentist soon and get it fixed, and then you'll be as beautiful as ever."

Mama kissed my forehead a second time, and then we made dinner together and talked about how we would tidy up the store.

You were too tired to join us for dinner again, Malka, and only wanted to stay in bed and sleep, as if you'd rather live with your eyes closed than be awake.

I know you are suffering. I know you miss Govorovo. I know it hurts to not have Bubbe with us. But I worry you will wither away if you don't let go of your sadness.

With my love forever,
Esther

HAVANA

February 4, 1939

Dear Malka,

Today was such a happy day. You woke up hungry, went to the kitchen, and got yourself a thick slice of challah slathered with butter and sprinkles of sweet Cuban sugar.

Until today you refused to wear anything but your woolen dresses from Poland. But after breakfast, you put on the green dress I made for you. And you slipped on the sandals from Zvi Mandelbaum, sandals like mine, with all your toes showing.

It was Shabbos. Papa and Mama and our brothers had gone to shul for an early-morning service before coming back to open the store. I was on the balcony watering the plants, and you came and said, "Look at me!"

"Malka, you look so beautiful! The dress fits you perfectly and it really does match the color of your green eyes!"

"You sewed this dress yourself?" you asked.

I could see how you enjoyed the way the dress swirled as you moved.

"I did," I replied. "I designed it and I sewed it."

"You are good. No wonder Mama is proud of you."

"Thank you, Malka."

Then you said, "Maybe I can help. Bubbe taught me to embroider flowers. I could embroider flowers on the dresses."

"What a great idea! Those can be our special dresses!"

We hugged each other, and although you were still light as air, your feet stood firmly on the ground now. We were becoming real sisters again, the way we had been in Poland.

"Esther, I want to start reading the letters you wrote to me."

"That's so wonderful, Malka! Let me get them for you."

I ran to our bedroom and brought out the old accounting notebook from Poland where I'd been writing my letters to you.

"How about if I read a letter aloud, then you read a letter aloud?"

"Yes, Malka! Yes!"

After we read the first two, you turned to me and said, "Sister, you wrote all these letters just for me?"

"Yes, I did. I missed you so much. And writing was a comfort for me too. I felt like I was talking to you across the distance and preserving new memories. It was like gathering seashells along the shore to keep them from being washed away."

We went back to reading the letters and were so entertained sitting in the rocking chairs and reading aloud to each other that we didn't notice when the key turned in the lock and Mama and Papa and our brothers returned home.

"Good Shabbos!" they called out from the entryway.

I quickly closed the notebook and hid it under my seat,

since we both wanted to keep our letters secret. "Good Shabbos!" we called back. "We're sitting here by the balcony!"

Papa's eyes shone when he saw you sitting with me, and Mama said how nice you looked in the green dress and the sandals.

Then I said to Papa, "We're going to need embroidery thread in every color. Malka is going to make special embroideries for our dresses."

"That is good, very good," Papa said. "I will give you all the thread you want, happily."

For the first time in days, Papa's furrowed brow relaxed and I heard him utter a prayer of thanks under his breath.

With all the love
a sister can give,
Esther

HAVANA

February 5, 1939

Dear Malka,

Last night, after our Shabbos dinner, I made sour cherry tea for all of us. The tea cheered us up and made us think Poland wasn't so far away.

"It reminds me of Bubbe," you whispered.

And Papa said, "May it be God's will that we see her again soon."

As I drank my tea in the beautiful teacup decorated with flowers and flying birds that was Francisco's gift to me, I was filled with memories of Agramonte and my happy days there.

Mama asked where I got the Polish tea, and I told her, "From our friends in Agramonte who have a store that sells foods from all over the world."

Then, Malka, you perked up and said, "The owner's name is Juan Chang and his nephew's name is Francisco Chang. And Esther made other friends too—Manuela, and her father, Mario José, and her grandmother Ma Felipa, and Doctor Pablo, who helped Papa when he was hurt, and Señora Graciela, who cries for her daughter, Emilia, who died."

"How do you know all this?" Mama asked with a puzzled look.

"Esther told me about them. I wish I could meet them," you said, and gave me a playful wink when nobody was looking.

Then I dared to ask our father something I didn't dream he would agree to. "Papa, would you let me take Malka to Agramonte tomorrow? It will be Sunday, so I won't miss school."

"By yourselves you'll go?"

"I know the route. We went many times, Papa. Remember?"

"Of course I remember. How could I forget?" He smiled and looked at you tenderly. "Would you like to go, Malka? Maybe you will enjoy the fresh air."

"Yes, I want to go!" you replied, with such enthusiasm, we were shocked.

Mama became concerned. "Is it safe for the girls to go on the train?"

Papa told her, "Our girls will be safe, I have no doubt."

This morning you held my hand, and together we rushed to the train station and arrived in enough time to grab two seats right next to the window. You kept your face pressed against the glass the whole way. You seemed to want to memorize the Cuban countryside and bring it inside you.

You pointed to the tall trees brushing the sky and asked, "Are those the Cuban palm trees?"

"Yes," I said. "They are palmas."

"How beautiful they are," you replied, and for the first time in days, you smiled.

When we arrived in Agramonte, you took a deep breath, and I said to you, "It smells sweet, doesn't it?"

You said, "I have never smelled anything so sweet."

"That's the smell of sugar. Azúcar. They grow a lot of sugar here."

"The work is bitter, but the result is sweet," you said.

"Malka! You remember those words from my letters!"

You smiled. "Yes, I do. Those were Papa's words. Now they're my words."

"Come," I told you. "Let's visit everyone."

We crossed into town and right away bumped into Señora Graciela. She was wearing the dark blue dress I had sewn for her.

"Am I imagining things?" she said in a merry voice. "Esther, what brings you here? And who is this pretty girl with you?"

"This is my sister, Malka," I told her. "We came so she could see Agramonte."

Señora Graciela was so happy. She insisted we go to her house right away. There was Doctor Pablo, reading the newspaper as always. "Terrible news, terrible news," he muttered. He pushed his glasses back up to the bridge of his nose, smiled at us, and said, "Esther, you grace us with your presence again."

Señora Graciela told him, "And this pretty girl is her sister."

They asked us to sit on the sofa under the portrait of their daughter, Emilia. On a big silver tray, Señora Graciela brought us sweet pineapple juice and toasted bread with mango jam and thick slices of cheese. You ate with gusto, dear Malka. That was a delight after all the days you've forced yourself to swallow your food.

I took you across the street and showed you where Papa and I lived during the year we were saving up enough money to bring all of you to Cuba. Then I led you to the store and there, as usual, was Juan Chang sitting behind the counter, waiting for customers. Francisco was sketching in his notebook.

"You haven't forgotten about us!" Juan Chang said. He asked about Papa, and I told him he was well and that Mama and our brothers had arrived safely.

Francisco smiled and turned his notebook around so we could see what he had been drawing. It was a ship at sea filled with people. "I hope refugees will always be able to come to Cuba and find a new home," he said.

"I hope so too," I said.

I told him I liked his sketch, and he gave it to me. "Take it, Esther, but promise you'll come visit us again."

Juan Chang didn't want you to leave empty-handed, dear Malka, and he reached around to the shelf behind him and pulled down a tin of the sour cherry tea. I was embarrassed to accept this generous gift again, as much as we all loved it, but he insisted we bring it home to Mama and Papa and our brothers.

And then, for the first time, Malka, you uttered a word

aloud in Spanish. You said, "Gracias," and it sounded so beautiful coming from you.

We went on to Ma Felipa's house. Manuela was putting the laundry out to dry on the clothesline. I saw that she was hanging up the dresses I had sewn for her and Ma Felipa. I called to her, "Manuela!"

"Esther, you're back! And that must be your sister!"

She rushed over and hugged us both. And, Malka, that was when you said your second word in Spanish. "Hola," you said. It was pure happiness to hear it.

"Guess what?" Manuela said to me cheerfully. "I'm going to secondary school in Jagüey Grande! I am learning so much."

I could imagine her a few years from now teaching the schoolchildren in Agramonte. How wonderful that would be!

Manuela brought us inside, and Ma Felipa embraced us with warm hugs.

After giving us each a glass of cool water from Yemayá's fountain, Ma Felipa offered us the coconut treats she makes. "This is delicious," you whispered to me.

Mario José was nearby in the fields, and Manuela ran to get him. He brought sugarcane for you to taste, Malka. You bit into it and smiled. "Azúcar," you said.

Outside in the yard, you saw the ceiba tree and you went and threw your arms around its wide bark, and you began to cry.

I explained to Ma Felipa about your sadness. "Triste, muy

triste, mi hermana," I said, and I didn't need to say anything more.

Ma Felipa and Manuela sang softly, "Yemayá Asesu, Asesu Yemayá," while Mario José gently tapped out the soul of the tune on his large batá drum.

After a while, you stopped crying. The sadness lifted and your green eyes glowed again.

"Esther, I am here," you said.

"I've missed you, Malka. I'm glad you made it."

On the train ride back to Havana, you looked at me with eyes still glowing and said, "I want to read the rest of your letters. Can I read them tonight, dear sister?"

"They are for you," I replied. "Welcome to Cuba."

From ESTHER,
with love

A NOTE FROM THE AUTHOR

THE MORNING of Friday, August 31, 1939, was an ordinary market day in Govorovo, Poland. The sun shone on the cobblestones. Children played tag, enjoying the late-summer warmth. Peasants from the surrounding villages arrived with wagons filled with grains and livestock, while Jewish residents had boots, clothes, and hats to sell. But there was tension in the air. Soon they'd know why.

The next day, September 1, 1939, a German bomb fell on Govorovo. The war had begun. Some of the Jews fled to Russia. Those who stayed were awoken eight days later by German soldiers shooting Jews who refused to come out of their houses. It was a Saturday. They shoved the Jews into their old wooden synagogue, telling them, "It is your Shabbos, go!" and set the shul aflame. Several managed to escape and survive. Nearly all who remained in Govorovo would later perish in the Holocaust.

I didn't know this history when I was a young Cuban immigrant girl growing up in New York a few decades later. But I was very close to my maternal grandmother, Esther, who was born in Govorovo. She had been an immigrant twice—to Cuba and then to the United States. We communicated in Spanish with a sprinkling of English, though Baba's mother tongue was Yiddish, of which she'd only passed on a few words to me.

I had noticed that Baba kept a black-and-white photograph on the wall of an old woman with a faraway gaze. One day I asked who she was.

"That was my grandmother," Baba told me. "She refused to come to Cuba with the family. She was very religious and was afraid she'd have to give up her traditions in Cuba. Instead she perished in the Holocaust."

Baba told me nothing more, but I will never forget that moment. This book was born then, though I didn't sit down to write it until many years later. And although much of Esther's story and her letters are fictional, many of the facts surrounding her are based on my family history.

I often heard Baba proudly tell the story of how she'd convinced her father, my great-grandfather Abraham Levin, to let her be the first of her siblings to join him in Cuba. This tropical island had become a haven for numerous Jews fleeing Poland's worsening economic situation and growing anti-Semitism on the eve of the war. It was thanks to Baba's courage—crossing the ocean alone and starting anew in Cuba—that her mother and siblings were saved from the horror to come.

Baba was older than Esther is in this book, but she still had to persuade her father that, though she was a girl, she could work as hard as her younger brother Moshe. She left Govorovo and arrived in Cuba in 1927 to find her father was working as a peddler. Peddling was a common way to make a living if you were starting from nothing, and my family started from nothing in Cuba.

My grandmother Esther lived to be ninety-two and was lucid until the end. Throughout her life, she was haunted by the loss of the grandmother she couldn't save. The framed photograph on the wall was a reminder of the sad fate of those who weren't able to start a new life in a new land and perished in places they once called home.

Baba never had any interest in going back to see Govorovo. Eventually I went on my own and tried to imagine Baba living there when she was young. But more than setting foot in Govorovo, what helped me to conjure the home she had to leave was the memorial book for Govorovo, also known as a Yizkor book. These books exist for many Jewish towns, or shtetls, that once were an integral part of the social landscape in Poland. They preserve the memory of Jews who lived there, refusing to let them fade into oblivion. Baba treasured the memorial book for Govorovo, which my great-grandfather helped edit. I learned about the destruction of the town in 1939 through the Yiddish reminiscences in the book.

One of Baba's younger sisters suffered from depression, though they didn't use that word at the time. They knew she was sad, desperately sad. I thought about that great-aunt, whom I found to be so thoughtful and sensitive, and wondered what it would have been like to move to Cuba as a young girl, knowing you were leaving behind your beloved grandmother. I gave

Malka all those feelings, that trauma, to contrast her with the brave Esther, always ready for a challenge.

We are all familiar with the immigrant stories of European Jews who passed through Ellis Island on their way to becoming Americans. I loved Karen Hesse's *Letters from Rifka* and thought I would tell a parallel story about a Polish Jewish girl searching for her America in the Cuban countryside. I wanted readers to know about Jews like my grandmother who found refuge in the "other América."

My grandmother made Cuba her home because racist and anti-Semitic quotas set in motion by the Immigration Act of 1924 restricted Jewish immigration from Southern and Eastern Europe to the United States. There were Jews who stayed temporarily in Cuba, treating it as a stopover until they could somehow manage to get to the United States, the "real America." But Jews like my grandmother fell in love with Cuba and hoped to stay forever. Then, in the 1960s, Baba, like many others, was disheartened to have to leave Cuba when the revolution turned Communist, and she lost all that she had worked for.

Most Jews who settled in Cuba felt liberated from the anti-Semitism they had felt in Europe. Yet scholars and writers have focused on one particularly distressing chapter of Jewish-Cuban history—the tragedy of the *St. Louis* vessel. This luxury liner brought 934 German Jewish passengers to Cuba who sought refuge from the Nazis. But upon arriving on May 27, 1939, only a handful were allowed in. Due to a rising tide of

Nazi sympathies among a powerful Cuban minority who used the press to advertise their hateful views, the ship was ordered out of Cuban waters. Refused entry to the United States and Canada, the SS *St. Louis* returned to Europe. About a third of the passengers found refuge in Britain. The rest were taken in by countries that soon found themselves under Nazi occupation, and some 254 of them died in concentration camps or at the hands of the Nazis.

Even though Cuba wasn't solely to blame for the tragedy, this "voyage of the damned" has loomed large in Cuban history. I believe this is because it seems so out of character for a country in which it is rare to encounter anti-Semitism. Cuba is a place of huge diversity, where people of different cultures and backgrounds coexist, and where Jews, in particular, have felt and continue to feel a sense of belonging. The *St. Louis* incident was a dark chapter in Cuba's history. That is what makes it so disturbing. In writing this novel, I wanted to imagine what it was like for my grandmother and my other family members to have arrived in Cuba on the eve of the *St. Louis* and found refuge while others, Jews like them, were later turned away.

Havana in the west and Santiago de Cuba on the eastern end of the island had the largest number of Jews. In those cities, there were synagogues, Jewish schools, Yiddish theaters, and Sephardic associations. But it's not generally known that there were many Jewish immigrants who also lived in the countryside, far from fellow congregants. Baba and her family settled in Agramonte when they first arrived in Cuba and were the only Jewish family in the town. Though called "los polacos," they felt they'd found a safe harbor on the eve of the war. So safe that once reunited in Agramonte, my great-grandfather Abraham had the peace of mind to write down all that he remembered of his youth in Poland in an old accounting book. This memoir, handwritten in Yiddish amid the swaying palm trees of Cuba, spoke nostalgically of the Jewish world he had lost. In a sense, my great-grandfather never arrived in Cuba; he left his heart in Poland.

But Baba fully and absolutely embraced her new Cuban life, which is why I chose to write from her point of view. Listening to her stories about Agramonte when I was growing up lit a spark in me. I knew I'd have to see Agramonte with my own eyes one day. The story that made an especially strong impression was about the real Doctor Pablo, who lived in Agramonte and was a friend to Baba and her family. In the late 1930s, Baba said, he organized a group of women and taught them first aid in case the Nazis invaded Cuba. Baba, of course, was proud to be one of the women who would assist Doctor Pablo, if called upon, and I was struck by how the impending sense of Nazi terror even reached Cubans living seemingly far away in the countryside. We were all tied together in the knot of history. That realization stayed with me and found its way to the heart of this book.

In addition to being a children's author, I am a cultural anthropologist, and so I felt compelled to do some fieldwork and historical research in the town of Agramonte. Luckily, there are excellent ethnographers and local historians in Agramonte who are keen to preserve their history and culture. That was how I learned about and visited the house with a fountain of water inside its walls that is dedicated to the deity of Yemayá. I went to see the sugar mills in the area, all abandoned today, and asked about the lives of the people who were once workers in the cane, among them many descendants of enslaved people. Haunting legends recalling the days of slavery took root among the people of Agramonte and nearby villages, a region known as Cuba's Little Africa. There is a bembé for San Lázaro every year, and I've been privileged to attend a few times, hear the ancient batá drums, and see the weeping ceiba tree with the chains around its trunk.

As I wrote this book, the different stories meshed—the Jewish-Cuban immigrant story and the Afro-Cuban post-slavery story. I tried to do justice to both and to conjure the thoughts and dreams of a young Polish Jewish girl landing in a town in the Cuban countryside that had preserved so many African traditions. Through my research, I learned there were Chinese Cubans living in Agramonte as well and realized that to tell this story, I had to include their voices too. I hope I did that with the sensitivity it deserves.

Although the Esther of this book is a fictional character, she represents many real young people of the past and the present who have crossed borders and shouldered responsibilities that only an adult should have to take on. As Esther states in one of her letters, "In times of emergency, a child must rise up and act older than her years." Today, there are brave young people from many places rising up on behalf of all of us, not just to make the world a better place but to be sure the world continues to exist.

While not precisely my grandmother Esther's story, I tried to capture her curiosity and passionate need to understand others. The vibrant spirit of Cuba, the kindness and generosity of its people, and the resilience of its culture gave her a newfound sense of freedom and hope for the future. My grandmother became Cuban before she became American, and I did too, thanks to her. I am forever grateful she chose to go to Cuba. There she learned to love life after losing so much. Her memory is a blessing to me. May it also be for readers of this book.

The author as a child in Cuba with her grandmother Esther, the inspiration for the book, and her grandfather Maximo.

RESOURCES

I HAVE BEEN fortunate to be able to spend many years researching the stories of the Jews of Cuba. To write this novel, I also drew upon inspiration and historical insight gained from the work of many scholars and writers. Here are a few recommended titles for further reading.

Children's Novels

Margarita Engle, *Tropical Secrets: Holocaust Refugees in Cuba* (New York: Henry Holt, 2009).

Alan Gratz, *Refugee* (New York: Scholastic, 2017).

Karen Hesse, *Letters from Rifka* (New York: Henry Holt, 1992).

Lois Lowry, *Number the Stars* (New York: Houghton Mifflin Harcourt, 1989).

Cuban History and Literature

Alan Astro, ed., *Yiddish South of the Border: An Anthology of Latin American Yiddish Writing* (Albuquerque: University of New Mexico Press, 2003).

Ruth Behar, *An Island Called Home: Returning to Jewish Cuba* (New Brunswick, NJ: Rutgers University Press, 2007).

Margalit Bejarano, *The Jewish Community of Cuba: Memory and History* (Jerusalem: Hebrew University Magnes Press, 2014).

Armando Lucas Correa, *The German Girl: A Novel* (New York: Atria Books, 2016).

Robert M. Levine, *Tropical Diaspora: The Jewish Experience in Cuba* (Gainesville: University Press of Florida, 1993).

Kathleen López, *Chinese Cubans: A Transnational History* (Chapel Hill: University of North Carolina Press, 2013).

Joseph M. Murphy, *Santería: African Spirits in America* (Boston: Beacon Press, 1993).

Fernando Ortiz, *Defensa cubana contra el racismo antisemita*, por la Asociación Nacional Contra las Discriminaciones Racistas (*Revista Bimestre Cubana* 44, no. 3, June 1939): 97–107.

Leonardo Padura, *Heretics* (New York: Farrar, Straus, and Giroux, 2017).

Felicia Rosshandler, *Passing Through Havana: A Novel of a Wartime Girlhood in the Caribbean* (New York: St. Martin's Press, 1983).

Jewish History

Gur Alroey, *Bread to Eat and Clothes to Wear: Letters from Jewish Migrants in the Early Twentieth Century* (Detroit, MI: Wayne State University Press, 2011).

Hasia R. Diner, *Roads Taken: The Great Jewish Migrations to the New World and the Peddlers Who Forged the Way* (New Haven, CT: Yale University Press, 2015).

Jack Kugelmass and Jonathan Boyarin, *From a Ruined Garden: The Memorial Books of Polish Jewry* (New York: Schoken Books, 1983).

Alice Nakhimovsky and Roberta Newman, *Dear Mendl, Dear Reyzl: Yiddish Letter Manuals from Russia and America* (Bloomington: Indiana University Press, 2014).

ACKNOWLEDGMENTS

Letters from Cuba exists thanks to my extraordinary editor, Nancy Paulsen. A year and a half ago, in the spring of 2018, I told her the story of my brave and stubborn grandmother Esther, who helped her father, my great-grandfather, bring the family from Poland to Cuba on the eve of the Holocaust. Without a moment's hesitation, Nancy said, "There's your next book." I was thrilled to be given that assignment. But could I write it? Knowing Nancy wanted the story gave me the atrevimiento, the chutzpah, to try. Somehow, in a whirlwind of teaching and travel, this book got written. Nancy was the kindest, most thoughtful and meticulous editor, sharing every moment of the journey with me. I am in awe of Nancy's work as an advocate for children's literature and feel so blessed to have been graced by her wisdom.

I am equally blessed, hugely blessed, to have Alyssa Eisner Henkin as my agent. Her loving support gave me the strength to stay focused during moments when the writing became overwhelming. I am grateful for her generosity, her vivaciousness, her willingness to hop on the phone and talk things through. I feel very lucky to be working with her and the expert team at Trident Media. Thank you to Alyssa for her faith in my storytelling and for helping me fulfill a dream I'd almost given up on—of being a writer. It's truly never too late to start, and having someone as brilliant and caring as Alyssa be your guiding spirit is pure joy.

Writer-friends whom I hugely admire were there for me, and I thank them with a full heart. Thank you: To Ann Pearlman for reading an early draft and giving me hope. To Reyna Grande for incisive comments that pushed me to go deeper into the relationship between Esther and her mother. To Marjorie Agosín for her compassionate reading. To Richard Blanco for poetry, friendship, and laughter. To Sandra Cisneros, who read what I thought was a final draft and showed me where it still needed work, teaching me respect for the written word that I will always be grateful for.

A group of amazing friends who are Cuba experts read earlier drafts and gave me comments that helped make this book better. Thank you: To Teofilo Ruiz for illuminating the history of Cuba. To Margalit Bejarano for sharing her knowledge of Jewish immigration to Cuba. To Jesús Jambrina for a profound literary reading. To Alfredo Alonso Estenoz, a native of Agramonte, for opening his home to me there many years ago and connecting me with his wonderful family, as well as for his insightful comments. To Eduardo Aparicio for making sure the Spanish flowed smoothly in the text. To Martin Tsang for crucial comments on the representation of Chinese Cubans and Santería rituals. To Lucía Suárez for a sensitive reading that helped me feel confident about the ending of the book. To Rosa Lowinger for caring about this story.

As a cultural anthropologist, I need to experience places, not simply imagine them. This book found inspiration in a 2006 trip to Govorovo (Goworowo in Polish). My former student, Erica Lehrer, a superb scholar of Poland, kindly accompanied me on this trip, opening my eyes to a country that had once been home to my grandmother and many other Jews. During that trip, thanks to the monumental research of Anka Grupinska for Centropa, I had the good fortune to meet Yitzhak Grynberg, a native of Govorovo living in Warsaw, who remembered my family and shared insights about what life had been like there before the war. Later I was fortunate to learn about the work of Stanley Diamond, who founded Jewish Records Indexing–Poland and, together with other devoted scholars, has unearthed extensive information about the Jews of Govorovo and neighboring towns and villages. I was fortunate to be able to turn to Mikhl Yashinsky for lyrical translations from the Yiddish of the Govorovo memorial book, which helped me to enter into the poetics of a disappeared Jewish world.

I went to Agramonte for the first time over twenty-five years ago, curious to see with my own eyes the place where my grandmother and her family lived after arriving in Cuba from Govorovo, the place also where my mother and my aunt Sylvia spent their early childhood years before moving to Havana. Growing up hearing all the stories of Agramonte, I expected it to be a mythical town, and indeed it is. Agramonte is an anthropologist's dream, filled with friendly people who take pride in their cultural heritage. I want to offer a special thank-you to Carlos Félix de Armas Samá, Rosa Arencibia Estenoz, Vitalia Arencibia Estenoz, Yoan Landa Arencibia, Suleidis Sanabria Acosta, and Tania Teresa Sanabria Fernández.

It was a delightful surprise to learn about Jill Flanders-Crosby's research on Arará social memory in Agramonte and Périco, thanks to my correspondence with Jonathan Mark (JT) Torres. He put us in touch, and I thank him for that act of kindness as well as for his moving writing about this historic region. I am grateful to have traveled to Agramonte in 2017 with researcher Melba Nuñez and her husband, Miguel, sharing with them the experience of the San Lázaro/Babalú-Ayé rituals. Finally, I offer my deepest thanks to book-artist Rolando Estévez, who has taught me so much about the region of Matanzas (Bellamar, as he prefers to call it), both the city and the province, through his poetry and art and years of conversations. I feel blessed for my friendship with Estévez, which has led me to return many times to the red-earthed corner of Cuba where I have roots.

In Havana, the city of my birth, I owe a special debt of gratitude to the large-hearted woman who was my childhood nanny, Caridad Martínez Castillo. She died last year at this time. I wish she could have read this book. She welcomed me to Havana when I began returning years ago and made me feel like Cuba was still my home. I am grateful for the warm welcome

I always receive from Consuelito Azcuy Díaz, my parents' old neighbor in Havana, and her daughter, my childhood friend Cristy Hernández Azcuy, and their lovely family. I want to thank historian Gerardo Hernández Bencomo, who knows everything about the history of our beloved Habana. Thank you to Adriana Hernández Gómez de Molina, who shared her knowledge of 1930s attitudes toward Jews in Cuba. Many dear friends have shared their Havana worlds with me over nearly three decades of return trips. Warm thanks to poet Nancy Morejón and artist Rocío García. And a big thank-you to Adela Dworin, who safeguards the memory of the Jews of Cuba.

Working with the book-loving team at Penguin Random House is an honor, and I am grateful for all the support I've received from everyone in the educational and marketing departments. Many thanks to Cindy Howle, Carla Benton, and Allyson Floridia for excellent copyediting. Special thanks to Elyse Marshall for being an amazing publicist. And a warm thank-you to Sara LaFleur, always a pleasure to work with, for expert assistance during every phase of the bookmaking process.

Thank you to all the librarians, teachers, booksellers, and young readers who opened their hearts to me as a writer and motivated me to write another book.

Thank you to John Parra for the beautiful cover artwork. The image conveys perfectly the hope and lightness of heart that Jewish immigrants felt when they set foot in Cuba as conditions grew very dark in Europe.

Thank you to the University of Michigan for supporting my work throughout the years and for providing funding for research trips to Poland and Cuba.

Thank you to PJ Our Way for an Author's Incentive Award, which provided support for my writing at a crucial moment.

Thank you to Petra Moreno in Ann Arbor, who sews gorgeous tango outfits and gave me wonderful pointers on how dresses are made so I could better understand Esther's sewing wizardry.

After choosing the title for my book, I learned that two previous nonfiction books, from 1844 and 1906, had used the title *Letters from Cuba*, and that the playwright Maria Irene Fornes had written a play also titled *Letters from Cuba* that premiered in 2000. I acknowledge these previous works and am glad to be in their company.

This story is in memory of my maternal grandmother Esther. I owe so much to Baba. If even a touch of her personality breathes through these pages, I will be content. As the oldest grandchild, I was privileged to get to know her well and loved her dearly. But she was a beacon for my entire maternal family, and I thank them all for keeping her in their memories.

A big thank-you, of course, to Mami y Papi, my parents, who have never forgotten about Cuba and our history on the island and have shared so many of their stories with me.

I am infinitely grateful to my husband, David, who's there for me always, besides being an incredible in-house fact-checker. My son, Gabriel, I cannot thank enough for all the joys and blessings he has given me. I thank Sasha, his wife, for joining our family and bringing more joys and blessings to us. Having two young artists in the family is a huge inspiration and has helped me to be a better writer.

And Cuba . . . Can you thank a country? As I was about to turn in the final version of this book, I felt a huge need to be in Cuba. I was fortunate to be able to finish *Letters from Cuba* in Havana, emailing with my editor, Nancy Paulsen, from a park bench a few blocks from where I grew up, connecting to the public Wi-Fi while birds sang and children ran around playing tag. To be back at the source of this story, in the place that gave my family the chance to survive, the chance to be alive, was such a beautiful gift. Gracias a la vida. To life, to life, l'chaim. Gracias, Cuba.

Ruth Behar

December 17, 2019

(Día de San Lázaro)

I am not dumb

When we lived in Cuba, I was smart. But when we got to Queens, in New York City, in the United States of America, I became dumb, just because I couldn't speak English.

So I got put in the dumb class in fifth grade at P.S. 117. It's the class for the *bobos*, the kids who failed at math and reading. Also in it are the kids the teachers call "delinquents." They come to school late and talk back and are always chewing gum. Even though they're considered the bad kids, most of them are nice to me. "Here, Ruthie, have some Chiclets!" they whisper and pass me a handful.

We aren't supposed to chew gum in school, so we hold the Chiclets in our mouths until we go outside for recess. Then we chew the Chiclets to death and stick the gook on the bottom of our desks when we come back inside.

Most of the kids know I'm in this class because I'm from another country, not because I really belong there. Or maybe I do belong there? It's been eight months since school started and our teacher promised I wouldn't be in the class for long.

I am not dumb. I am not dumb. I am not dumb . . .

The first time I worked up the courage to raise my hand in class was a few weeks after we had arrived from Cuba and I was wearing flip-flops instead of shoes and socks like the other kids. But when our teacher, Mrs. Sarota, called on me to answer the math problem, I didn't have the words to say the number in English.

"Well, Ruth?" she asked, staring down at my bare feet. "Do you know the answer or not?"

I froze and a few kids laughed at me. But not Ramu.

He's not dumb either. Ramu is in our class because he's also from a different country. He comes from India and was raised there by his grandmother, who only speaks a language called Bengali. His parents came to New York first, and after they made enough money, they brought Ramu and his little brother, Avik, here.

Ramu has picked up English faster than I have because his parents know English and force him to speak it at home. Mine are always yelling, *"¡Habla en español!"* Especially Mami, who can understand a little English, but is usually too embarrassed to try to speak it.

Ramu is skinny and bows his head when anyone talks to him. I'm his only friend and that's because he lives down the hall from us on the sixth floor of our apartment building. Ramu brings Avik to school and I bring my brother, Izzie. Our little brothers are in the same kindergarten class. But after school Ramu and Avik rush straight home. Mrs. Sharma doesn't let them play with the other children.

Their apartment smells different from ours. I get whiffs

of it whenever we stumble into each other on the way to school. Today when Ramu and Avik stepped into the hall, Izzie and I were waiting for the elevator, and I asked, "What is that perfume?"

"It's my mother's curry," Ramu says.

"What's curry?"

"A spice. It makes everything taste good, even cauliflower."

"That's amazing."

"Yes, it is. And my mother burns sandalwood incense. She says it's good for meditation and the spirits like it too."

"Spirits?"

"People who used to be alive, when they're not alive anymore, become spirits. My grandmother says they are all around us. We can't see them but they watch over us. Of course, spirits don't eat, but they can smell fragrant things like curry and incense."

During lunch at the cafeteria, Ramu offers me something from his lunch box, a pastry filled with mashed potatoes his mother made.

"It's a samosa," Ramu tells me. "Maybe you'll find it too spicy."

Some kids at the table pretend to hold their noses. One says, "It smells like sweaty armpits!"

"No it doesn't!" I shout back.

I take a slow first bite. It tastes like a *papa rellena*, a crispy stuffed potato my nanny Caro made for me as a snack in Cuba. Eating Ramu's samosa makes me feel like Caro and Cuba aren't so far away.

"It's real good! Thanks, Ramu."

Ramu gives me a shy smile. "Very glad you like it."

I beg Mami to make *pastelitos de guayaba* after Izzie and I get home. The following day, I give Ramu one of the sweet pastries at lunch.

"The filling is guava fruit. I hope you'll like it," I tell him.

Ramu eats it slowly without saying a word. When he's done, he finally says, "I like guavas. We have them in India too," and I sigh.

"And do you have mangos in India?"

"Oh yes, drippy sweet mangos."

"Just like in Cuba!"

"I don't just miss the mangos," Ramu says. "I miss being able to go outside and play with friends. My mother worries too much about us. She doesn't let us do anything by ourselves."

"I know what you mean. In Cuba, even when I was five years old, my mother used to let me take a taxi all by myself to go visit my aunt Zoila, who used to sew pretty dresses for me. Can you imagine?"

"Yes, here everything is different," he says, with a faraway look in his eyes.

"But maybe one day we'll both get to taste mangos in India and Cuba!" I say, trying to cheer him up.

"Oh, Ruthie, I like that you have such an imagination!"

Ramu and I sit together every afternoon after lunch period so we can practice our English.

Our favorite story is "The Princess Who Could Not Cry," about a princess who is placed under an evil spell and forgets how to cry. She laughs at everything, even sad things. When they toss away all the toys she loves from the tallest tower of the castle, she laughs, even though she feels terrible.

A little ragged girl arrives and announces, "I've come to help the princess cry."

The queen tells her, "Promise me you won't hurt my daughter."

The little ragged girl curtsies and replies, "I promise, Your Majesty, I will bring no harm upon your daughter. I just want to help her."

She goes into a room with the princess and draws two onions out of her bag.

"Let's peel these onions," the little ragged girl tells the princess.

As the little ragged girl and the princess pull apart the layers of the onions, the tears start pouring from both their eyes.

That is how the princess learns to cry!

The evil spell is broken, and the little ragged girl and her poor mother are given a nice house next to the castle where they live happily ever after.

"That is the best story!" I say to Ramu as we finish reading aloud.

"Yes, it's very fine," he replies. "Very fine indeed."

"Ramu, you always talk such a fancy English."

"Like they do in England. It's the Queen's English, you see."

"Yes! And now we live in Queens!" I say, joking.

"Very charming, Ruthie. That's almost funny."

"Let's ask Mrs. Sarota to test us!" I tell Ramu.

"But will you ask her, Ruthie, please? You see, in India, we don't talk to the teacher unless the teacher talks to us."

"Okay, I will ask. I'm not afraid of the teacher."

Mrs. Sarota comes to our desk and I say, "Me and Ramu are ready to switch into the smart class."

"In English, we say 'Ramu and I.' 'Me and Ramu' is incorrect."

I don't lose my courage. I repeat, "Ramu and I are ready to switch into the smart class."

"Is that so, young lady? Both of you?"

"Yeah, Mrs. Sarota," I reply, trying to keep from giggling. Mrs. Sarota wears her hair in a big bird nest on top of her head and today it's lopsided.

"Very well, young lady. Which of you can spell the word 'commiserate'?"

Ramu gets it wrong, but I get it right—two *M*s and only one *S*.

She doesn't ask, but I also know what the word means. To "commiserate" is to feel sorry for somebody else's bad luck.

"Very good, Ruth. I agree you're ready to be promoted. But remember to say 'yes' rather than 'yeah.' On Monday, you can join the regular fifth-grade class."

I see Ramu gazing sadly toward the floor. It's not fair. He's much better at English than I am. He talks like the Queen of England herself.

"Please, Mrs. Sarota, can you give Ramu another chance? Give him a harder word and see if he can spell it. Please."

Mrs. Sarota's eyes suddenly sparkle. "You said the magic word, 'please.' Ramu, can you spell the word 'souvenir'?"

I would have gotten that word wrong, but Ramu knows how to spell it right.

"Excellent job, Ramu. You are also promoted," Mrs. Sarota says. "On Monday, you and Ruth can join the regular fifth-grade class."

"Mrs. Sarota, you are very kind," Ramu says in his most polite voice.

Ramu gives me one of his shy smiles and that is enough of a thank-you for me.

I knew I wasn't dumb. I knew Ramu wasn't dumb either.

It's Friday. After the weekend, when we come back to school, both of us will be in our new class with the smart kids.

Yippee!

I collect my schoolbooks and say good-bye to the other kids. One of them looks sad that I'm leaving and gives me some Chiclets. "You may need them!"

I wish all the kids could come with Ramu and me to the smart class. I don't think any of them are really dumb. They just find school boring. They'd rather play all day.

In a chorus they call out, "Bye, Ruthie! Bye! Study hard or they'll send you back here again!"

go-go boots

The buildings on our street are made of old bricks and they all look exactly the same. If you don't know the number of your building, you're lost. My brother, Izzie, and I know our building by now, but we still walk home together from school, holding hands, as if we'd got to New York only yesterday.

The lawns have gone from snowy white to blotchy brown to a hopeful green color, and dandelions are sprouting on them. I wish I could run barefoot in the grass the way I did in Havana. There was a park nearby that had giant banyan trees that you could lie under and curly grass that tickled your toes when you ran through it. But most of the lawns here have wire fences around them that will cut your fingers if you touch them and signs that say "Keep Off the Grass!"

We are near our building when a girl named Danielle calls out, "Ruthie, Ruthie," and catches up with us.

Danielle is from Belgium and acts very sophisticated. She has silky black hair that reaches to her shoulders and flips perfectly. She looks like she could be on TV. With my messy ponytails and dress from the bargain basement, I feel like the fairy tale's ragged girl with the basket of onions when I'm around Miss Mademoiselle Danielle. Today she has on a lace-trimmed beige blouse and a pleated blue skirt. And she's wearing new go-go boots. Black go-go boots! She also just arrived in New York, but they put her in the smart class because she speaks French *and* English.

"Do you want to play hopscotch?" Danielle says.

"Yeah," I reply. "I always want to play."

"Très bien," she says and smiles. Danielle crosses the street, walking so elegantly in her black go-go boots to a building as drab and dreary as ours. Before she disappears, she turns and waves. "See you out here in a minute!"

Izzie and I race each other to see who gets into the elevator first. I get there a second before him and press the button for the sixth floor, and as the door closes, we are panting and breathless. We can't wait to change out of our school clothes and go out and play. We have the whole weekend. No school till Monday.

Yippee!

As soon as we step into our apartment, I can smell the sweet rose scent of Mami's Maja soap, which comes wrapped in tissue paper with a picture of a Spanish flamenco dancer in a red-and-black gown, and Papi's Old Spice, which he splashes on his cheeks before going to work.

Mami is waiting for us at the door and gives us a hug and a kiss. She always looks so pretty, as if she's going to a party. She's wearing her clothes from Cuba—a polka-dot dress with buttons down the front and a wide leather belt—and she's got her high heels on, and red lipstick. "A wife has to look her best when her husband comes home," she always says.

"Mami, you got lipstick on me!" Izzie yells, wiping the stain off his cheek.

"I'm sorry, *mi niño*. It's just that I'm always so happy to see you," she tells us in Spanish.

Mami points to the dining table, set with two grilled cheese sandwiches and two glasses of chocolate milk.

"We just want to go out and play!" Izzie complains.

"If you don't eat, you'll faint," Mami tells him. *"Se van a desmayar."*

We gobble up our sandwiches and chug down our milk while Mami stands over us trying to get us to slow down. *"¡Niños, no se apuren tanto!"*

But nothing can keep Izzie and me locked up in the house while the sun is shining. We jump up from our seats, change into our play clothes, and rush to the door. I remember to grab some chalk and toss it into my jacket pocket.

Mami stops us and reminds us not to be home late. Our hands must be clean and we must be smiling and ready to kiss Papi the minute he walks in the door or he gets angry.

Off we go, finally!

Izzie says, "I'll race you! I'll run down the stairs and you take the elevator!"

"Okay, Izzie! Let's see who gets there first."

Sure enough, Izzie gets to the first floor just as the elevator door opens.

"Wow, you did it, Izzie!"

My little brother looks so proud of himself. He's cute with his crooked bangs and missing front teeth.

"Now let's see if I can beat the other boys at tag. They're really fast," he says, sounding worried.

"You will, Izzie, you will."

And he scurries off to "the back," an alleyway behind our row of buildings where the boys chase each other for hours and hours.

Blue and pink chalk in hand, I claim the sidewalk in front of our building for my hopscotch board. I bend down to sketch out the squares for the game and add flowers at the four corners.

When I look up from drawing, Danielle is there.

"What a pretty hopscotch you're making, Ruthie!"

Danielle is still looking so stylish in her fancy school clothes. Isn't she worried she'll get them dirty? Won't her mother scold her then? But what makes me the most jealous is that Danielle is still wearing her black go-go boots! And I have on my old sneakers, with the holes forming around my big toes.

I've been begging Mami for a pair of go-go boots ever since seeing the blond lady on TV wearing them and singing that song "These Boots Are Made for Walkin'." And I can't stop humming that catchy song:

These boots are made for walkin'
And that's just what they'll do

One of these days these boots
Are gonna walk all over you!

Now Danielle, looking so grown-up in her black go-go boots, announces, "I'll go first!"

Ava and June, who live in the building next door, come to play with us. They are plain American girls. They only speak English. They never dream about a lost beautiful island. They are surprised when they hear me talking Spanish with Mami.

"Why do you talk another language?" they ask me.

"Because we're from Cuba, that's why."

"Oh," they reply, and don't know what else to say.

They stare at Danielle as she hops from square to square on the hopscotch in her go-go boots, light as air.

I'm not light like Danielle, but I am strong, and I get two squares farther up on the hopscotch.

Danielle doesn't mind at all. She smiles and says, "Very nice, Ruthie! You are excellent at hopscotch! You are Miss Hopscotch Queen of Queens!"

She says the word "hopscotch," extending the *shhhh* sound at the end of the word with a French accent and it sounds glamorous.

Ava and June take turns after Danielle and me. The four of us keep on playing one round after another. I can throw the stone farther and leap higher than Danielle, Ava, and June. Yes, yes! I am Miss Hopscotch Queen of Queens! Yippee!

We don't stop playing until the sky grows dark and loses all its blueness.

I'm happy being Miss Hopscotch Queen of Queens.

But I still wish I had go-go boots.

"Guess what, Danielle," I say.

"What, Ruthie?"

"I'm moving to your class on Monday."

"Really? *C'est magnifique!*"

Those words just roll off Danielle's tongue. Then she glances at her watch. She's the only girl I know who wears a watch and the wristband is a gleaming gold bracelet.

"Excuse me, my friends, I must go. My mother is expecting me for dinner."

She skips away in her black go-go boots and halfway down the block she turns around and smiles at me and says, "Bye, *chérie*, bye, bye."

Praise for
LUCKY BROKEN GIRL

"Reading *Lucky Broken Girl* feels like meeting a courageous new friend who will be with you forever. Ruth Behar succeeds at infusing her tale of heartbreak and suffering with a glorious celebration of forgiveness and hope."

—Margarita Engle, author of *The Surrender Tree*

"A powerful story of fortitude and courage that will remain in the hearts of young readers."

—Marjorie Agosín, author of *I Lived on Butterfly Hill*

"In the shadow of tragedy, Ruthie finds the light of love and optimism. Although it indeed takes a village to raise a child, her story of resilience and triumph reminds us that sometimes it takes a child like Ruthie to raise a village."

—Richard Blanco, author of *The Prince of Los Cocuyos: A Miami Childhood*

"*Lucky Broken Girl* takes us into a world that is at once deeply familiar and astonishingly new—the world of young people negotiating English as a second language, of families being forced from their homelands, and of friendships across cultural divides. But most of all, it is the world of Ruthie, an unforgettable character whom I grew to love and cheer for."

—Jacqueline Woodson, author of *Brown Girl Dreaming*